F
Sh6c

63921

| DATE DUE | | | |
|---|---|---|---|
| May 12 72 | | | |
| | | | |
| | | | |
| | | | |
| | | | |
| | | | |
| | | | |
| | | | |
| | | | |
| | | | |
| | | | |

GAYLORD M-2    PRINTED IN U.S.A.

# CONTRABAND OF WAR

DICK P. HOCKING LOOKED DOWN AT LAST UPON APPADACCA.

[*To face p.* 23.

# CONTRABAND OF WAR

## A TALE OF THE HISPANO-AMERICAN STRUGGLE

BY

## M. P. SHIEL

AUTHOR OF

'THE MAN STEALERS,' 'THE YELLOW DANGER,'
ETC.

WITH ILLUSTRATIONS BY A. J. PEARSE

THE GREGG PRESS / RIDGEWOOD, N. J.

First published in 1899 by Grant Richards
Republished in 1968 by
The Gregg Press Incorporated
171 East Ridgewood Avenue
Ridgewood, New Jersey U.S.A.

Copyright© 1968 by
The Gregg Press, Inc.

Library of Congress Catalog Card Number: 68-23727

Printed in United States of America

# AMERICANS IN FICTION

In the domain of literature the play may once have been the chief abstract and chronicle of the times, but during the nineteenth and twentieth centuries the novel has usurped the chief place in holding the mirror up to the homely face of society. On this account, if for no other, the Gregg Press series of reprints of American fiction merits the attention of all students of Americana and of librarians interested in building up adequate collections dealing with the social and literary history of the United States. Most of the three score and ten novels or volumes of short stories included in the series enjoyed considerable fame in their day but have been so long out of print as to be virtually unobtainable in the original editions.

Included in the list are works by writers not presently fashionable in critical circles—but nevertheless well known to literary historians—among them Joel Chandler Harris, Harriet Beecher Stowe, Thomas Bailey Aldrich, and William Gilmore Simms. A substantial element in the list consists of authors who are known especially for their graphic portrayal of a particular American setting, such as Gertrude Atherton (California), Arlo Bates (Boston), Alice Brown (New England), Edward Eggleston (Indiana), Mary Wilkins Freeman (New England), Henry B. Fuller (Chicago), Richard M. Johnston (Georgia), James Lane Allen (Kentucky), Mary N. Murfree (Tennessee), and Thomas Nelson Page (Virginia). There is even a novel by Frederic Remington, one of the most popular painters of the Western cowboy and Indian—and another, and impressive minor classic on the early mining region of Colorado, from the pen of Mary Hallock Foote. The professional student of American literature will rejoice in the opportunity afforded by the collection to extend his reading of fiction belonging to what is called the "local-color movement"—a major current in the development of the national belles-lettres.

Among the titles in the series are also a number of famous historical novels. Silas Weir Mitchell's *Hugh Wynne* is one of the very best fictional treatments of the American Revolution. John Esten Cooke is the foremost Southern writer of his day who dealt with the Civil War. The two books by Thomas Dixon are among the most famous novels on the Reconstruction Era, with sensational disclosures of the original Ku Klux Klan in action. They supplied the grist for the first great movie "spectacular"—*The Birth of a Nation* (1915).

Paul Leicester Ford's *The Honorable Peter Stirling* is justly ranked among the top American novels which portray American politics in action—a subject illuminated by other novelists in the Gregg list—A. H. Lewis, Frances H. Burnett, and Alice Brown, for example. Economic problems are forcefully put before the reader in works by Aldrich, Mrs. Freeman, and John Hay, whose novels illustrate the ominous concern over the early battles between labor and capital. From the sweatshops of Eastern cities in which newly arrived immigrants toiled for pittances, to the Western mining camps where the laborers packed revolvers, the working class of the times enters into various other stories in the Gregg list. The capitalist class, also, comes in for attention, with an account of a struggle for the ownership of a railroad in Samuel Merwin's *The Short-Line War* and with the devastating documentation of the foibles of the newly rich and their wives in the narratives of David Graham Phillips. It was Phillips whose annoying talent for the exposure of abuses led Theodore Roosevelt to put the. term "muck-raker" into currency.

While it is apparent that local-color stories, the historical novel, and the economic novel have all been borne in mind in choosing the titles for this important series of reprints, it is evident that careful consideration has also been given to treatments of various minority elements in the American population. The Negro, especially, but also the Indian, the half-breed, Creoles, Cajuns—and even the West Coast Japanese—appear as characters in various of these novels or volumes of short stories and sketches. Joel Chandler Harris's *Free Joe* will open the eyes of readers who know that author solely as the creator of humorous old Uncle Remus. And there is a revelatory volume of dialect tales, written by a Negro author, *The Conjure Woman* by Charles W. Chesnutt.

In literary conventions and the dominating attitudes toward life, the works in the Gregg series range from the adventurous romance illustrated so well by Mayne Reid or the polite urbanity of Owen Wister to the mordant irony of Kate Chopin and the grimmer realism of Joseph Kirkland's own experiences on bloody Civil War battle-fields or the depressing display of New York farm life by Harold Frederic. In short, the series admirably illustrates the general qual-ities of the fiction produced in the United States during the era covered, just as it generously mirrors the geographical regions, the people, and the problems of the times.

PROFESSOR CLARENCE GOHDES
*Duke University*
*Durham, North Carolina*

December, 1967

# PREFACE

The Spanish-American War, which marked a turning point in American history — our emergence as a world power through the acquisition of the Philippines, Puerto Rico, and Guam — produced practically no significant literature. Stephen Crane's stories, the accounts of Richard Harding Davis, and Frank Norris' articles from *McClures Magazine* are read occasionally today. But their works cannot be compared with those which came out of the Civil War, the two great Wars of the twentieth century or even the Viet Nam War. Elbert Hubbard's *Message to Garcia* (1899) sold forty million copies, but is today a literary curiosity in the same category as the *Farmer's Almanack*. The giants of American literature were preoccupied with other problems and themes.

*Contraband of War,* the best contemporaneous novel dealing with the Spanish-American conflict, was written by an Englishman, who was born in Montserrat, West Indies, and who was never able to reproduce the intonations and turns of phrase which separate the speechways of the Englishman and the American. This story, with its superhuman protagonists, its intrigue of high finance, and duels fought with all of the then-advanced resources of technology, bears an obvious resemblance to a James Bond thriller, but with two major differences: the total absence of sensational sex (this was the Victorian Age) and the symbolic roles of the antagonists as representatives of two opposing civilizations and sets of values. Bond's heroes are cool and detached scoundrels in spite of their protestation of loyalty to England, America, the Free World, etc. Shiel's Dick P. Hocking, whom the author modestly calls "one of the shrewdest fellows in the world," is a vulgar, brutal speculator with the physique of "a Brobdingnagian paperweight," whose only passion is self-aggrandizement, and who possesses to a high degree the ability to identify without hypocrisy his own lust for power with the march of civilization. Only Schulberg's Sammy Glick could have a thicker skin or a more schizophrenic split between means and ends.

Hocking is the owner of large sugar and tobacco estates in Cuba. Any weakening of Spanish power would be of great benefit to him, so "He plumped for war, or at least for a war-scare," using his influence with McKinley to push for American involvement. Thus, John Hay's "splendid little war" is seen as a matter of speculative profits in commodities, specie, and bonds; not as the heroic struggle for Cuban independence proclaimed by the Hearst yellow press. Hocking, like Jay Gatsby, is the child of his age, and could only appear in an era of mad speculation and reckless expansion. And Shiel, like Fitzgerald, has the ambivalent attitude of the romantic toward a creation which is blatantly predatory and ugly. There is something sturdy, heroic, and glamorous about this rhinocerous-like man to whom war and peace are matters of indifference as long as the market fluctuates the right way, which it inevitably does.

Shiel, the son of a parson, also creates the secondary character of a machiavellian parson named Petersen who aids Hocking in his nefarious ventures, and who can at a moment's notice provide elaborate arguments for the superiority of Anglo-Saxon civilization and the God-ordained necessity for its dominion over the lesser races.

. Hocking's arch-enemy is a fantastic Castilian bearing the equally fantastic name Appadacca — also rich, but self-indulgent to the point of decadence. Appadacca is seconded by a priest who, like the Reverend Petersen, provides his master with the intellectual rationalization for the supremacy of Old Spain and Spanish Catholicism. The Cubans, like today, play the role of pawns caught in the machinations of two superstates.

*Contraband of War* is no masterpiece. It is crude, romanticized, and marred by a Hollywood ending. But it is powerful in imagination and symbolism, damned good fun to read, and most important, it is virtually the only contemporaneous imaginative work which we can turn to for an insight into the events of the Cuban rebellion of 1896.

F. C. S.

# CONTENTS

# LIST OF ILLUSTRATIONS

# Contraband of War.

## CHAPTER I.

### A GENTLEMAN OF SPAIN.

DICK P. HOCKING weighed, stark naked as he was born, just thirty-two stone.

When he put his left hand behind his back, and cocked out his thick, short right leg at Wall Street, with the intention of sending the biddings up, and by hook or by crook of 'getting there,' you saw solidity. He was a sort of monument in flesh, conveying a tremendous suggestion of heaviness. He did not look like a man; he was like a Brobdingnagian paper-weight.

His right leg was not really short, as we have said; he was, in reality, a tall man, only he looked squat in proportion.

His two jaws seemed to hang on his shoulders.

In addition, he carried a broad, thick beard, and above his superfluously large body a small bullet-head, flat behind, of which the hair was always cut as short as a convict's.

His face was not an ugly one ; it was only a distinctly vulgar one, like everything else about the man.

He was one of the shrewdest fellows in the world. Sometimes, early in the morning, he would leap out of bed, blow through a whistle in his bedroom, send his hoarse, rasping voice through a tube, and do a deal that would set New York and Throgmorton Street talking for a week.

When he took a dislike to a broker, to a fellow-speculator—and Dick P. Hocking was apt to take strange dislikes—it was, in general, woe to that broker or speculator. He had once suddenly appeared on 'Change, and, off his own bat, sent up three months' fine paper $2\frac{1}{2}$ per cent., for the purpose of smashing an operator who had unconsciously thwarted him in a Greek Monopoly deal.

It was admitted that the price of silver was a matter depending on the will, or the whim, of Dick P. Hocking. In Washington his back-stairs influence was enormous ; for who did not know that Hocking, at a critical moment, had

thrown his huge weight into the McKinley scale,
and that had it been otherwise, things might
have been otherwise also?

This powerful man, for whom the world, like
some golden (or silver) palace, seemed to have
been specially built, had a thorn in the flesh.
Other rich men, to show that perfect happiness
is not for man on the earth, suffer from weari-
ness, from anxiety, from disease. From all this
Dick P. Hocking was exempt. But he suffered
from the thorn in his flesh.

This thorn was called Immanuel Appadacca.

Immanuel Appadacca was a man whom Dick
P. Hocking had never seen. Yet Hocking
hated him worse than poison.

The man whom Hocking had seen, and
whom for a long time he thought he hated, was
Josef Campos. Then, quite suddenly, by a
mere chance, he got to know that Campos, the
visible, was only the hand, the agent, of Appadacca, the invisible.

So often had Hocking been crossed and
whipped and outwitted by this unseen power,
this mysterious *deus ex machina*, that at last it
might be said that the one remaining object of
his life was to destroy it.

Who was Josef Campos? Everyone knew.

Who was Immanuel Appadacca? No one could say.

The two known facts about Appadacca were these—that he must be fairly rich ; and that he possessed the swiftest ship in which a man had ever crossed upon the deep.

Now, it happened that, about six months before the outbreak of the war between Spain and the States, one Señor Canalejas, a Spanish Minister of Justice and of Finance, had come to the States, and in an interview with the President at Washington, had been told that the desire of America was to see an autonomous government in Cuba, and assistance given to the ' Reconcentrados '—though, of course, the States recognised the sovereign rights of Spain —nothing more.

The interview, however, got abroad. And the consequence of this hint of the President's was an immediate slight slump in ' Spanish' on 'Change everywhere, quotations going down from $57\frac{1}{8}$ to nearly 55. And the next day Josef Campos was reported to be realizing largely in Mexican Internals, Peruvians, and American Railways.

To meet pressing liabilities? It was an inference !

Hocking snapped his doughy fingers.

Spanish bonds, then, were the weak point of Immanuel Appadacca.

It was not certain, but he was in the state in which men jump at conclusions. It was at least a hint of light in the absolute darkness which had tormented him for seven years.

He already possessed in Cuba considerable territories of tobacco and cane estates. And that night Dick P. Hocking slept in a Pullman, bound for Washington.

He plumped for war, or at least for a war-scare—and he had enormous power.

If he had not a right to determine how Cuba was to be governed, who had?

In the exciting months that followed down crept 'Spanish' on every Bourse in the world. They reached 45; they reached 40.

And the more Dick P. Hocking and a whole train of smaller men under his thumb plumped for war, the more isolated became the position of Josef Campos, and the more guessable his embarrassments.

But whosesoever was the brain that inspired him, Campos was well inspired. On February 23, when the anticipation of trouble and the fear of dear money had already led to a heavy fall in high-priced securities, Josef Campos at three o'clock suddenly disposed of a large handful of South American steamships, which were promptly ̤taken up by Hocking ; and the whole of the funds realized by Campos were in half an hour invested in Argentine railways.

During the evening the news reached New York that a boat of the Rio-Buenos Ayres line had been mysteriously sunk — by Valparaiso buccaneers, it was said ; and the immediate consequence on the opening of 'Change was a slump in South American steamships, and an unwonted activity in the land-traffic market. By the *coup* Campos realized two millions, and Hocking sunk five, and took it badly.

It was anticipated now that Josef Campos would not hesitate to dispose of the evidently large amount in Spanish bonds which he held. These were daily sinking lower, and it was assumed that so shrewd an operator, seeing the heavy selling from Paris, and probably himself in touch with the Spanish Government, could not remain blind to the rotten financial position of Spain.   But Josef Campos sold not a single Spanish bond.

'Suppose I believe in them ?' he said to a financier friend, who wondered at his pertinacity.

'But——'

'I have that right, you know.   Every man

must judge with his own eyes. Besides, I am the servant of another.'

'Ah—in that case. But could you not advise your chief of the patent facts?'

Campos smiled. He was a tall, thin man, with a brown face and silver-white close-cut hair, though he had not reached middle age. His beardless face was handsome, his manners distinguished, his eyes dark-blue and restless.

'No,' he said, when his smile was over, 'I never advise my chief.'

Yet in his heart he was anxious: confident, in the long-run, in the unfailing brain on which he relied, but anxious for the near present. Again and again, by the receipt of secret information, for which it was impossible for others to account, he was able to startle the market during February, March, and the beginning of April, with successful deals. And yet he was like a man whose backbone is touched with disease—as a financier, he had locomotor ataxy.

'Spanish' was his backbone: and 'Spanish' was going, going.

Then he did what he had said that he never did, *he advised:* and he received an answer which he remembered to his dying day.

The next day he received a message from

the ex-Queen Isabella, stating that, on the
Spanish side, war had definitely been decided
upon.   This was on April 12.   He at once sent
the information to Appadacca.

Appadacca wired :

'You are very simple.   Please discover date
of sale of land on Guiana-Venezuela frontier by
Calvos.   Want to buy.   Make private offer.'

Campos knew that the vast piece of ground
in question was in the market, or would shortly
be ; but he rubbed his eyes.   The land was of
no present value, it would require many millions
of money to develop its resources ; even if his
chief was able to purchase, his fortune was in
no condition to be 'plunged' in wild specula-
tions of that sort.

But he did not hesitate.   He at once attended
at the branch firm in Brooklyn, to hear that the
Calvos would in no case part under 5,000,000
dollars ; but probably would not part at all
except by way of public auction.   However,
the branch telegraphed to the head firm at
Caracas that an offer had been made by Appadacca.   And by night Richard P. Hocking
knew of it.

Now, Hocking had no conception of the
motive of Appadacca in aiming at the acqui-

sition of this particular tract of ground ; but he knew two things : that Appadacca had never yet, on any single occasion, allowed himself to be out-bidden in any object which he desired ; and he knew that the business concern represented by the names of Campos and Appadacca must fall, if pushed.

He determined to bid, to push ; it was of no importance to him how high.   For the money sunk he even had a plan how to recoup himself.

He was a connoisseur in ships, was Dick P. Hocking.    His thousand-ton composite yacht was a luxurious thing, capable of twenty-three knots, and good for the eye to look upon. But she had been designed by hirelings, and the *Huelva*, which he had once seen in Boston harbour, had been designed by the brain of Immanuel Appadacca.

This ship had seemed to him dainty as a tender lily looking up in surprise at the world from the water-side ; lying at anchor in the sea, she conveyed the impression of a young doe the moment before it starts, affrighted, into running.

To put his hands into his pockets, and bulge his broad hips into a greater breadth on the deck of that ship, Dick P. Hocking thought would be a good thing.

And there were precious few things in this world desirable in his eyes which, in the long-run, he did not possess.

He brooded so continuously in secret over this whim that in the end his eagerness to walk the deck of the *Huelva* took equal place with his eagerness to crush the man who had so often cost him dear.

But though on pleasure he was bent, he had a frugal mind. War was coming; whoever else did not know it, *he* knew it very well. America wanted ships, and was buying them; and how good a thing would be the *Huelva* to America in that day! He reckoned on his fingers the millions which she would fetch.

He would charter her to the Government, he promised himself; he would not sell her.

He made a bid by telegram of six millions for the Venezuela-Guiana territory, and this lay for some days on the files of the firm of Calvos.

He had had many friendly relations with the firm, and now, guessing his motives, they did him a good turn—and themselves also. They telegraphed that bidding was likely to be brisk; that it was rumoured that Immanuel Appadacca had suddenly appeared at his castle among the mountains west of La Guayra. He was likely, therefore, to be present in person at the auction; so that nothing less than the personal presence of Dick P. Hocking, or of a fully authorized agent, in the auction-room, would be likely to secure him the territory in question.

Hocking looked about him, rushing through a limited area of New York in quest of certain knowledge. Had Campos sold any ' Spanish'? No. At what were ' Spanish' now? As low as 38. Had he time? Yes—he had even two days to spare.

He telegraphed to the *Union* at Raleigh Bay, and on alighting from his train at St. Augustine in Florida, met her there. That ponderous bulk could travel, being light and full of motion.

And now events developed rapidly.

First, there came the settled conviction of the public that nothing could avert war; active preparations began in the States, mobilization of troops and militia, registration of volunteers both for army and navy, and the purchase of ships ; then the squabble between the Houses ; truculent and imperious messages from the President to the Spanish Government ; the break-out of a definite war-fire in long-sleeping old Spain ; then the resolutions of Congress ; and the signed ultimatum.

' Spanish ' fell to $37\frac{1}{8}$.

## CHAPTER II.

IT was true that Immanuel Appadacca was at his Venezuelan château.

He was writing a Spanish madrigal in an apartment overlooking the sea at three in the afternoon of April 20, when an ivory card, scribbled with the words, 'The *carrosse* awaits your Excellency,' was dropped through a slit in the porphyry wall upon a table near his hand. He glanced at it, and continued to write.

Here the hot sweltering sun came in in mellowed rays through blue and scarlet-tinted glass, making tolerable to the eye the blaze of splendour with which the apartment was adorned.

From the gaudy mosaic floor to the torrents of copper - coloured draperies that rolled in thick luxury from the entablatures, and the hundred ornaments of gold and ivory and malachite that crowded the not large apartment, there was poured forth a suggestion of princeliness that bewildered the imagination. A soft sound of music, the source of which was not visible, breathed through the apartment.

Far below lay, glittering in bright sunlight, a sheltered bay, readily accessible to the château by steps cut zigzag down the cliff side.

In appearance Appadacca was one of the most striking of men—pallid, with ink-black hair, but under the pallor a certain suggestion of duskiness which could not be readily fixed and described. Some remote ancestor had, in fact, been an Indian squaw, and this trace, mingling with the highest caste of the blood of Seville, still informed his wan visage.

He was rather below the middle height, with a well-knit, compact, erect figure.

The whole man was extremely finely wrought, beautiful in a high degree. Of his face, in moments of perfect calm, the riveting feature was the lips, well-chiselled, pale, and marble in the firmness of their pressure. When he spoke, it was the eyes that caught the attention : they lit up into a species of flaming dominancy.

He had been left rich on the death of his

father, but, tiring of a life spent wholly in seclusion and study, he chose to direct from his various palaces about the world what was known as the House of Campos.

In character, in thought, in aspiration, he was intensely Spanish.

At his name, the Queen Regent, the people in the inner circle of the Court, the Ministers, smiled with a certain mild indulgence. His ideas, like the ideas of all men somewhat above the crowd, had in them a savour of wildness.

The question which puzzled him always as a boy was this: *Why* was not Spain great among the nations? She *had* been!

She had still all the elements of greatness within herself — a large home-territory, rich in the good things of the earth; her sons were proud and nimble and brave; they had over-run and dominated the world. Yet now Spain had become a byword, a synonym for weakness.

Afterwards, he definitely fixed the origin and secret of this tragedy : Spain had been first made great, and then destroyed, by one of her own sons—Columbus.

He had discovered America, and old America had made Spain the mistress of the world, and new America has made her its reproach.

He saw clearly how this was so : Spain, in reality, was a maritime power, a colonizing force. To her, whose sceptre once stretched over the earth, and whose sons gave their names to continents, there now remained Cuba and the Philippines.

Still, from the Rio Grande del Norte to Cape Horn, all that great world of Central and South America was, in feeling, Spanish, or Portugo-Spanish—in feeling, in speech, in habit, in instinct.

And at the thought of the ultimate destiny of that great continent, even when a boy with ripening thought he shuddered.

Instead of beautiful old Spain of the hidalgos, the Monroe doctrine ; instead of the mellow and musical reign of great Ferdinand, the encroaching paw of Dick P. Hocking.

Absorption of the beautiful by the ugly, slow but sure—this was Destiny.

Later on he began to find pleasant the dream of a greater España, strong at home, and once more a continent abroad. The dissipation of the little republics of South America, and their aggregation into one vast flourishing Spain—it became his vision.

He had seen all the world. His learning, his beauty, his gaudy and mysterious way of life, had made him a chief figure at courts, at masques, in secret cabals, in the conclaves of revolutionists. From China to Chili he had investigated the world : and nowhere had anything struck his imagination as being so beautiful as Spain, or as being so ugly as—'the States.'

The passion of his youth was for the beautiful ; its detestation was for the ugly.

Though a Spaniard (Venezuelan by birth) his motive was not patriotism. It was something greater—his ideal of the beautiful.

He conceived that nothing whatever was of half so much importance to the actual world of the nineteenth century as the conservation of the small residue of the humanly picturesque which remained to it.

When the Venezuelan dispute arose, he bitterly resented the interference of America; England encroached, but the United States encroached still more in raising her voice to check the encroacher. She had, he thought, no right to raise it.

The outbreak of the Cuban War opened his eyes to one fact—that the chief misery of Spain was her impecuniosity.

Poor nations can no more command the respect of their colonies than poor men of their servants. Cuba broke from her leading-strings mainly because they were fustian.

And now his vague dreams all at once froze within him into definiteness. What was wrong he saw ; and how it could be remedied he saw also.

At this time he devised the *Huelva*.

She was a craft of 12,500 tons, of steel and wood, having a belt of Harveyized nickel-steel, as though made for the express purpose of warfare.

During the period of her building, the ship had been what she was destined to continue— an enigma.

Was she a yacht, or a ship-of-war ? While she lay upon the stocks in the Union Ironworks of San Francisco, this had been the question of rare privileged sightseers.

The vague answer to these questions was that she was 'a composite vessel,' designed in person by a Venezuelan millionaire for his private use.

Some, looking at her lithe sheer, her entrancing suggestion of swiftness, said 'yacht.' Others pointed to an armour belt six feet deep, and three inches thick ; to five torpedo-tubes—one in the stern above the water-line, and four below ; to the complete armoured deck at the

water-level extending from stem to stern, two
inches thick on the flat part, five inches thick
on the slopes; and they promptly said 'sloop-
of-war.'

For the rest, she was constructed on the
usual system of double-bottom, connected with
watertight flats at stem and stern, thus extending the double-bottom to the extremities of the
ship.

If there were no visible guns, there were,
at least, visible on her main deck eight casemates, and on her upper deck six, armoured
with six-inch nickel-steel of the size usually
constructed for carrying four-inch quick-firing
guns, and fitted with the usual dismounting and
stowing gear.

As to these casemates, a singular contrivance
had been adopted. They had been made water-
tight on the inner as well as on the outer side.
The men, therefore, who crewed the possible
guns would be protected from explosive shells;
and also, should a gun-post get damaged,
between-deck spaces would be insured from the
irruption of water.

There was no part of the ship upon which
the minutest forethought, the adroitest cunning,
had not been lavished—and with forethought
and cunning, wealth.

Upon her engines, above all, an extravagance of care was expended in their manufacture, in their adaptation. The boilers, twenty-two in number, were of the latest type of Belleville, and the engines triple-expansion, driving twin screws. The thickness of deck over engines, boilers, and magazine-spaces was doubled.

On the day of her launch she lay upon the water a unique thing.

She combined the formidableness of a battle-ship with the buoyancy of a duck; she was the last triumph of shipbuilding; in the same entity was the lightness of foot of Asahel and the strength of Samson; she was force wedded to frivolity.

There was something almost secret about her building; there was something mysterious about her launching; there was something bizarre and unguessable about her movements.

She was manned by a crew gathered from nearly every region of the globe, gathered by Appadacca himself, and gathered under circumstances the most unexpected, the most outré. One of her stokers was a Chinaman, condemned to death for murder in Pekin, for whom Appadacca had purchased a substitute; another of the crew was a Cockney street gamin who probably owed his rather enviable position to a pair of brisk blue eyes; the captain was a Maltese Mediterranean coaster, a rough man of little education, yet a born sailor, who had fought side by side with Appadacca in a village fray among the Western Sicilian mountains; the first lieutenant was a nobleman of Andalusia, royally connected, poorer than Lazarus, prouder than Lucifer; three were Chilian contrabandists, chosen each of them at a different time, under quite different conditions, with varying motives; there were many races, Irish, Peruvian, half-caste, Catalan, Basque, Arab—but there was no American.

The only hint of nationality on board the ship was to be found in the fact that the predominant language was Spanish. By such men as those called by Appadacca from the world a language was readily learned.

The Cockney and the Chinaman swore at each other in Cockney and in Chinese, and obeyed in 'the language of the gods.'

Could anyone have looked into the hearts of this crew and seen how there the image of one man lay enshrined and worshipped, he would at once have arrived at some sort of conception of the strong personality which swayed them.

The movements of the ship, as of her master, were incalculable. At the hour of the blowing up of the *Maine*, the *Huelva* lay, without her master, in a creek outside Havana harbour; and half an hour after the explosion steamed away. Since then she had appeared neither in Spain nor at Taranto, where Appadacca owned a palazzo, nor at Venezuela.

Sometimes for weeks Appadacca buried himself in the gloomy luxury of a cabin, where a shimmering fleece of liquid-looking cloth-of-gold carpeting the floor mingled with paintings of David, and the uncouth grotesques of old Egypt, and the chaste carvings of Greece, in a rich bizarrerie of pomp ; his presence on board being at such times known only to the greater part of his crew by mouth-to-mouth rumour. Sometimes, again, she cruised for months without him.

Suddenly, on the very day when General Woodford left Madrid, and, at Washington, Señor Polo de Bernabe applied for his passports, the rumour spread through Caracas and La Guayra that the *Huelva* was lost.

It was the day when the stretch of land contiguous to the boundary line in dispute between Britain and Venezuela was to be disposed of at public auction by the Calvos. Some hours before the sale it was said that the wreck of the ship had been seen upon some rock-islands a long way down the coast, near Cumana.

The details were explicit; the news was eagerly discussed. If it were true, dark clouds must overshadow Appadacca's sky. Spanish bonds were at the lowest quotations yet reached.

Sharp at four the auction was timed to commence; and as the clocks struck, the buzz of the crowd in the room died suddenly into perfect silence. Appadacca entered.

The place was full, many people having come merely to get a sight of the face of this man. It was a third-rate apartment at the back of the Calvos office, without flooring or furniture, save a chair by which the auctioneer stood, and a table with writing materials.

It was a picturesque, somewhat squalid, gathering of men, quite Spanish-American in character — sombreros, ponchos, hide-boots, colours, dirt.

Appadacca wore a tunic of very thick plushy dark-blue velvet, with rough woollen stockings, and a wide hat, pinned with a dagger of gold, the rim rather concealing his face.

On his entrance the sale began without delay.

The auctioneer, in a hurried way, read out the specification, ending with the words : 'And now, gentlemen——'

By the side of the table stood an old man, the head of the firm of Calvos, and near him Appadacca, holding in his hand a bundle of script and title-deeds.

A hoarse, rasping voice was heard :

'I offer seven million pesos.'

Appadacca slightly nodded towards Señor Calvos.   He said :

'Eight.'

The crowd parted into a wide lane for the passage of a great bulk of flesh which now moved forward into the small open space.   The eyes of Dick P. Hocking looked down at last upon Appadacca as from a citadel.

Hocking said :

'Nine.'

And Appadacca said :

'Ten.'

Both were apparently calm, except that Hocking's chest and abdomen heaved somewhat largely in the taking of his breath.   Appadacca, as he callously raised the bid, figure by figure, in the merest whisper, examined one after another the papers in his hand.

Hocking put his left hand into the pocket of

his loose, enormous trousers, and he cocked forth his short-looking, ponderous right leg, and, fetching a breath from the gulf of his abdomen, he said :

'I offer eleven million pesos.'

And Appadacca, turning his leaves, in the merest whisper said :

'Twelve.'

'I offer thirteen million pesos,' said Dick P. Hocking.

Appadacca turned over the leaves of paper in his hand. There was a pause. He frowned a little. He said :

'Fourteen.'

'I offer fifteen million pesos,' said the emphatic, self-sure, gross voice of Hocking. With every bid his stuck-out right leg seemed to lift a little, and his huge body to come an inch more forward.

There was a pause again.

'Fifteen million pesos,' said the auctioneer—'fifteen million. Is there no advance ?'

Appadacca was very closely examining his leaves of paper now. His head bent over them. An eight-sided clock, hanging by a ring on the board partition, ticked half a minute—a minute.

'Sixteen,' came from Appadacca's lips.

' I offer seventeen million pesos,' said Dick P. Hocking, heaving his mountain of flesh yet an inch nearer.

These were huge figures. The roomful of people were on the very tiptoe of excitement. Spain and America were on the point of war ; and here, they had a sort of idea, were Spain and America ominously fighting out the big warfare in little, just as the old kings used to decide the issue between two armies by the single combat of two chosen champions.

Which would win—ugly, strong, nineteenth-century, Saxon Dick P. Hocking, with his encroaching, ponderous right leg, or picturesque, dainty, small-handed, Latin Immanuel Appadacca, turning the leaves of his papers with the dreamy old air of a medieval student of Salamanca ?

Certainly Hocking seemed the favourite of the gods. Appadacca now was looking too closely at his papers. Was he not—hesitating ?

' Seventeen million — going at seventeen——'

' Eighteen,' said Appadacca.

Down came Hocking's leg an inch nearer.

' I bid nineteen million pesos for this property,' quoth he.

And as he said it, Appadacca smiled.

He made a sign to the auctioneer that the bidding was not over, and at once he stepped up to old Calvos, the head of the selling firm.

'You, I think, are Señor Calvos?' said Appadacca, not even careful to lower his voice to a pitch inaudible to Hocking and the others near.

'Yes, señor,' said Calvos.

'Then I can speak to you;' and he smiled with ineffable condescension. 'The parcel of land which you are selling it is my whim to possess. I have now, however, it seems, bid my entire fortune—securities, châteaux, bric-à-brac, even the value of my horses. There is nothing left, señor, except one thing—my yacht, the *Huelva*. I offer to bid two million pesos more, on the understanding that you accept the *Huelva* at that sum, should no higher bid be made.'

'But—señor—the *Huelva* is—on the rocks!'

'She is afloat, señor.'

'She is wrecked!'

'She is now steaming toward Caracas at the rate of twenty-seven knots an hour, señor.'

'Can you believe that, señor?'

'Yes, señor.'

'But have you not, then, heard the report?'

'Ah yes—the report. The report is not a true report. The report has been spread abroad by that person, for his own purposes.'

He barely indicated Hocking with his head. Dick P. Hocking was like stolid wood, waiting.

'So you believe the *Huelva* is afloat?'

'Yes.'

'But with what motive could anyone——'

'You are not so simple, señor! With *this* motive : that, in case I should be compelled to offer her as a bid, the amount of my bid might be as low as possible, since I should be bidding a risk.'

'Is not the *Huelva*, then, insured?'

'No, señor.'

'Well, suppose I accept your offer, señor— say two million pesos?'

'You will do well, señor. She cost fifteen millions. She is worth fifty. And she should be steaming into Caracas at this moment—she *is*, in fact.'

'Well, it is agreed. You have the papers with you? And you will hand them over immediately, if the bidding falls to you?'

'Precisely so.'

'And there are no tedious formalities? The *Huelva* will be ours on the spot? The papers are duly regular?'

'There are no formalities. She will be yours

—as far as she can be anyone's other than
myself, señor.'

'What does that mean, señor ?'

'It would be long to explain, señor.'   He
smiled.   'May I now bid ?   I bid——'

Before he could name the figure, there arose
a bustle, a pressure, and a hubbub at the door ;
and a moment after the whole crowd of loiterers
broke into involuntary cheering.   Two idlers
of the town had come running with the news
that the *Huelva* had just dropped anchor in the
bay.

For three minutes nothing could be done.
The room was a babel of tongues.

Dick P. Hocking shifted his quarter-ton
weight from one leg to the other.   He was
embarrassed.

That Appadacca would now part with his
ship for two million pesos was not to be expected.   So far the Yankee's scheme had failed.

Old Calvos's face wore a look of dogged
shamefacedness.

'So much the better for you, señor,' he
said to Appadacca.   'The *Huelva*, then, is
here.'

'You said, señor——'

'So much the better for you.'

'Really ?   How ?   I do not see your meaning.'

' You will now, of course, demand more. Oh, I do not blame you !'

Appadacca's lip assumed the faintest curve of contempt.

'I demand nothing, señor. I had already arranged.'

' Oh—ahem!—well, that is only what one would expect from a gentleman. Yes. You adhere, then——?'

'Yes. May I now bid? I bid—twenty-one million pesos.'

Then there was silence.

The auctioneer looked at Hocking. Hocking looked at the ground. With an arm the size of most legs he made a slight deprecatory wave. The hammer came down.

The land was Appadacca's.

But the ship was Hocking's!

For, half an hour after Appadacca had handed the title-deeds to Calvos, Calvos handed them to Hocking, receiving in return a cheque for fifteen million pesos, and thus clearing thirteen millions by the deal.

Dick P. Hocking stood for an hour at the very end of a small jetty projecting into the bay, and his hands bulged his pockets. Not once did his gaze shift from the *Huelva*, lying there like a painted ship upon a painted

ocean.   She seemed to him like a doe the
moment before it starts, affrighted, into running
—and she was his !

He jerked his head sideward at her as he
turned to leave the jetty ; and he said :

' I guess you are the kind of hotel that will
put up Dick P. Hocking to-night, my girl.'

At seven he was sitting at a gleaming oval
table made of walrus-tusk arabesque in ebony
in the cabin of the *Huelva.*

Man after man of the crew, one by one, two
hundred and eleven, came up to him as he sat
there ; and from a hand-bag crammed with
Venezuelan gold pieces he paid them off,
adding a month's salary in lieu of notice.   He
possessed at times a certain large generosity
which even his enemies could not deny him ;
and till eleven in the night he was engaged in
this task.   Then, weary, he was led down three
corridors to Appadacca's chamber ; he turned
on the azure-blue jets of electric light ; he un-
dressed himself ; he drew on a suit of voluminous silk pyjamas that would have fitted an
elephant ; and he threw himself on the most
luxurious bed of which he had ever dreamed.
One by one he had warned the crew that by
nine, at the latest, the next morning they must
have left the *Huelva* to their successors.

HE LOOKED AT HER A MINUTE.

[*To face p.* 31.

At the moment when Dick P. Hocking began to snore with the vibratory resonance of a trombone, Immanuel Appadacca, at his château ten miles away, in Tunisian slippers, gold-embroidered, softly opened a door. He had in his right hand an antique gold candlestick, and to the shade of crimson silk which mellowed the light he added the shade of his left hand.

In an alcove, concealed by tapestries of black and crimson velvet, was a bed. Appadacca laid the candlestick upon an ottoman, and with exquisite caution drew aside the draperies. In the alcove on the bed lay in careless sleep a female.

She was a girl of seventeen; her bosom was half revealed; her masses of absolutely black hair lay far in vagrant largesse over the bed and pillows. He looked at her a minute; he stooped; he touched her forehead in the lightest caress with his lips. As he did so, he breathed the word ' Good-bye.'

Turning to move away, he glanced upon the lithe sleeping form again, and smiled faintly.

' Little Lola,' he said ; and, again, he added, ' Good-bye.'

He let the curtains fall together noiselessly as he passed out, and, with the light, went walking rapidly through the house.

In one chamber he selected a key from a bunch which he carried, and opened a cabinet. From this he took two cylindrical objects of the size and shape of an ordinary ruler.

He then ascended a narrow wooden stair to the flat roof of the castle. It was a luminous tropical night, the vault rich with stars; no moon. Appadacca looked abroad for a few minutes—over the mountains above him, down into the gloom of the still bay. The roadstead of La Guayra, on which lay the *Huelva*, was invisible to him.

He had with him a box of coloured fusees, and striking a fusee, he applied the flames to one of the two objects taken from the cabinet. Spouts of bluish sparks began to fizzle and shoot upward, and in another moment long ribbons of bluish flame went aspiring skyward from his hand, to burst in a cataract of bluish glamour three hundred feet above his head.

He put down the burnt-out rocket, and at once applied a flame to the other; and this time the night was lit up with a vermilion glow, ribbons of vermilion flame, and a bursting cataract of vermilion glamour in the sky.

It was a signal to the crew of the invisible *Huelva* lying in La Guara roadstead.

Having done this, Appadacca, without a moment's delay, descended to the suite which he occupied in the castle.

And now, for about half an hour, he busied himself in collecting papers, a cameo here, a small painting there, an ancient Limoges enamel, a cangiar of Tangiers. These he placed in a portable cabinet, which he locked.

He sounded a gong. A black servant appeared.

'Take this to the boat in the bay,' said Appadacca, indicating the cabinet.

And as the box left the room, he took from a rack a tiny Venetian stiletto, stuck it in his girdle of silk, and followed the servant.

They descended the steps in the rock to where the wavelets splashed languidly on a rough natural landing-place. There, in a highly-polished shallop, two men rested on their oars. The stern of the boat touched the rock. The negro deposited in her the box. Appadacca sat down in the stern.

Without a word from him, the oars lifted and touched the water, and the light boat leapt forward.

A quarter of a mile out burned the three very slowly-moving red port, green starboard,

and white mast-head lights of a steamship.    It
was the *Huelva*, which had dropped round
hither from La Guayra.

As Appadacca stepped upon her deck, he
said to her captain :

' The course is north by east, and the speed
twenty-eight knots.'

At once he disappeared into the cabin.

As the *Huelva* began to skip the waters with
the light step of a young grisette, he stood by
his bedside, meditatively gazing at the great
bulk of Dick P. Hocking, who, in spite of the
flood of light which now poured upon his face,
still slept and snored.

# CHAPTER III.

### DICK P. HOCKING LIFTS HIS ARM.

THE next day the two nations which had produced these two men were in a state of war.

At three on that day the *Huelva* dropped anchor at Ponce, in Puerto Rico.

The first lieutenant landed, and despatched this message by the Domingo-Cuba cable to Señor Sagasta, the Spanish Premier:

'Immanuel Appadacca requires letters of marque to use *Huelva* as privateer. Meanwhile will act on private authority of Queen. The *Montserrat* will be protected as far as Cienfuegos.'

The *Montserrat* was a Spanish transportship, which, since April 13, had left Las Palmas (Canary Islands) with a thousand troops, beside war material, stores, and money, for the Spanish forces in Cuba.

And in an hour the *Huelva* left Ponce, where she drained the town of coal, and steered directly west.

In a very small room in her cabin, a room which seemed scarcely big enough to contain him, sat Dick P. Hocking. An elbow was on a knee, and his fingers supported his forehead. He was very hungry ; his throat was dry. He touched an electric button.

Instantly there appeared before him a bowing Chilian rascal, with a number of parti-coloured ribbons round the sombrero which he held in his hand, and *botas vaqueras* reaching above his knees.

'Well, my lad, I guess you can roll your tongue about a bit of honest lingo, though I know a bit of yours, too,' said Hocking.

'I spoke already to your Excellency last night,' said the man, in decent English.

'Then you tell me this : does this man Appadacca mean to starve me on board my own ship ?'

'Not at all, your Excellency.'

'I don't see much victuals coming along this road, all the same, so far.'

'Your Excellency has only to order what you require,' said the Chilian, bowing low.

'Oh, I do the ordering, do I ? Well, suppose

you bring round a good roast chicken, as thick
as you like to make it, and a bottle of——
Have you got any lachryma Christi wine?'

'Yes, your Excellency.'

'Well, then, say a "good round capon"—
which is poetry—and a bottle of the lachryma.'

'Yes, your Excellency.'

'Then move.'

'I wait, your Excellency——'

'I see that.  But I do not want you to wait.
Why wait?'

'Payment must be made first, your Excellency.'

'This is a new sort of hotel, then, I calculate?

'No, your Excellency.  But such are my
orders.  Payment must be made first.'

And now, for the first time, some suspicion
of what was coming, some dim remembrance
of stories of extortion practised by the old
buccaneers and marooners, the Kidds, and
Morgans, and Averys, crossed the brain of
Dick P. Hocking.  He said:

'I have got little or nothing to pay with, my
lad.  Stop a bit—here's a greenback.  I guess
that will about do my day's board anyway.'

'The price of a fowl is five million dollars,
said the Chilian, 'and the price of a bottle of
any sort of wine is fifteen millions.'

And now Dick P. Hocking showed his race—its stoicism, its squareness to events, its genuine large-mindedness, exhibiting itself in a manner so commonplace and remote from display as to approach vulgarity.

This demand for the five million dollars meant, if it meant anything, that he was to be slowly and cruelly starved.    But he neither groaned nor showed surprise.

'Well, I don't call that a bad deal, my lad,' he said.    'No man knows better than Dick P. Hocking that business is business.    I make you an offer of four million dollars for a fowl, and fourteen million dollars for a bottle of lachryma Christi wine.'

'My orders, your Excellency——'

'Never mind your orders, sonny.    My turn may come some day, and—what is your name?'

'My name is Zambra Adelo, master.'

Dick P. Hocking took out his note-book from a vast breast-pocket, and he scribbled that name in pencil.

'Now, Zambra Adelo,' he said, 'look you, my son: I tell you my turn may come some day—may, mind you—I am not saying *will*— and I make you a bid of four million dollars for that fowl, and fourteen million dollars for that bottle of wine.'

'Your Excellency is wasting his breath,' replied Zambra.

'Very good, sir. What is the price of a loaf of bread on board this ship of mine?'

'Three million dollars, your Excellency.'

'Not dear, considering. Well, you bring me round a roast fowl, a loaf of bread, and a bottle of lachryma Christi wine, and don't stop to chew your spittle, neither.'

'If your Excellency will sign these three papers——,' said Zambra; and he laid the papers on a three-legged stool, and took pen and ink from a shelf.

Hocking, without hesitation, signed.

Now, a fowl, a loaf, and a bottle of wine were not an overpoweringly large meal for a man of Dick P. Hocking's cubicity. By nightfall he was hungry again; and when, before nightfall, the Chilian had come to clear away the *restes* of the meal, and had found a piece of loaf and some fragments of fowl, he had asked if he should take them away, for they were Hocking's; and Hocking had said: 'I guess so.'

Under that bulging paunch there lay a stomach more high, and a pride more unconquerable, than ever swelled beneath the courtly exterior of grandee or hidalgo.

At all events, the fowls and the wine became

a pretty frequent order from the captive
locked in the small room. The lowest rate of
living possible for Dick P. Hocking established
itself at the rate of twenty-three million dollars
a day.

On the evening of the 25th, just after sunset,
the *Huelva* sighted a large three-master to the
north-west, opposite the Cuban town of Trinidad;
and on running in toward the land for half an
hour, made her out as the *Montserrat*.

The war was by this time fairly under
way. Nothing heroic had, indeed, happened;
two Spanish merchant ships had been seized;
recruitment was going forward with considerable
zest in the squares of New York, and other
American cities; North Cuba and South-West
Cuba had been blockaded; the world was waiting for the first serious encounter between the
American Eastern squadron which had left
Hong Kong and the inferior Spanish force
assembled round Manila. Some war-vessels
had mysteriously left Cadiz bound west, and
excitement as to their unknown destination prevailed in New York. Also it was known that
the *Montserrat* was upon her adventurous way;
nor did anyone doubt that she must be inter-
cepted with her valuable cargo before reaching
Cienfuegos.

On the discovery of the identity of the *Montserrat*, the *Huelva* quickened her pace, and walked up rapidly on the other ship. At three hundred yards, the *Montserrat*, at a signal from the yacht, put out a boat, and her captain was rowed to receive Appadacca's instructions.

Appadacca, however, remained invisible. The captain of the transport spoke with the captain of the yacht in the cabin of the latter. And this cabin immediately adjoined one of the two apartments in which Dick P. Hocking, dozing most of the day in a sitting posture, dreamed of boiled and roast and stew.

He had now given notes of hand of over sixty million dollars for a few days' scarce rations.

Now, Hocking had started life as a clerk in a Chili nitrate office; he had all his life had large interests in Cuban and South American concerns; he had a very fair smattering of some Spanish patois somewhere in his cute and much-experienced head : so when he heard two voices in colloquy, and this question asked, ' How many American ships are blockading Cienfuegos?' he bent his ear much closer to the intervening door, and the musing, vacant eye of the listener was Dick P. Hocking's.

The answer was : ' Two cruisers, both nineteen knot boats, and crash for you if they get near you !'

It was the captain of the *Huelva* who spoke, a thick-bearded, brown, short man, with plain, thin hoops of gold in his ears.   He added :

' Here is a paper written by my master himself, telling you how you are to act hand in hand with the *Huelva*.   You will see that you are not really to go into Cienfuegos at all, but only to make a feint that way.   We are going to take in your stores and arms now, but not the men till the last moment.   The paper will tell you.   What we want to know from you is this : Is there anything in the way of prizes going on the seas the way you have come ?'

' There is,' said the other captain.   ' I had it from a Matanzas sloop in the Bahamas that a big transport would be leaving in four days— that should be to-morrow—from Key West for Havana, crowded with rifles and stores for the army coming to Cuba.'

' And her name ?'

' The *Sable*.'

' Convoyed ?'

' I heard no—alone.'

' Ah, we have her, then !'

' Something rich if you take her.'

' Good ! we take her.   But time, time, Señor

Capitan ! We need be in Cienfuegos by midnight. My master has conference with Gomez, the rebel chieftain.'

Dick P. Hocking heard no more ; nor did he know that all this concerned him personally. He put up his hands before his eyes, looked at them, and his mouth opened in a desperate yawn.

He was feeling intensely now the pinch of hunger, he, the opulent, the scatterer ; for on the day before he had nothing, nor on this day. Had he, then, ceased to satisfy his cravings for the sake of a few millions ? Not he. The fact was that he had no more millions to squander, there being a limit to all wealth. And Dick P. Hocking, with a certain rough honesty that was in him, had blurted the fact.

He had ordered his chicken, his wine, and his loaf. And when Zambra handed him the customary three papers, Hocking had said :

' Come, you just get me those eatables, young man. I guess " nothing " is about the name of what's left to pay you with.'

And the result, had he known the character of those with whom he had to do, was what he might have expected. He got no fowl, no wine, and no loaf. He lived upon the sight of his fat fingers ; he yawned till his jaws ached.

And larger grew the great empty hole within him.

About an hour after he had listened to the conversation in the apartment near, while he dozed with sideward-hanging head and opened mouth, the door opened. The captain of the *Huelva* entered.

'I am from his Excellency to you with a proposal,' said the man. 'Can you understand this talk of mine?'

'Some,' replied Hocking.

'Then here it is for you. His Excellency——'

'Who is his Excellency, my man?'

'Immanuel Appadacca.'

'Go ahead, then.'

'His Excellency has present need of sixty thousand dollars—a mere nothing—in specie, understand. Paper no good. In specie. Well, he means to put you in another ship to-night, if you agree, and get an order from you near the Florida coast for the sum ; and on receiving it, you have thenceforth what food you want— everything—free of cost and charge. You agree, I know.'

'H'm!  I don't say I do, neither.'

'You will.'

'You will starve me, you rascal?'

' Yes.'

' And if I fall into your views—you feed
me meanwhile—you give a famishing man
something to eat *now*, I guess?'

' No.   Everything after ; nothing first.'

' That means, I'm thinking, that I shall have
to fast for days, my man, doesn't it?'

' Some days.'

' But I tell you, I'm famishing already.'

' Can't help that.   Money first.'

' Yes, yes.   I guess I am a business man
myself.   Dick P. Hocking knows what business
is, and likes it.   But you are Christian people,
I reckon, on board this ship?   You belong to
a Christian race, I'm thinking——'

' Money first,' said the captain.

Dick P. Hocking looked the man slowly up
and down from the crown of his head to the
tip of his boots.   Then he put his hand into his
breast-pocket, drew out his leather note-book,
and said :

' Would you mind giving me your name, my
man?'

' My name?   That is nothing to the purpose,
señor.   My name is Silvio Murena.   Come,
now——'

' Silvio Murena,' said Hocking slowly, while
he inscribed the name — for future reference,

perhaps. ' I take it that you still refuse to give a hungry man a bit of food?'

' Come, you trifle, señor !'

For quite a minute Hocking said not a word. He sat regarding the floor, elbow on knee. Then suddenly he heaved himself upright, and out went his right leg, and up rose his mighty right arm; and with a high flush of wrath on his face, he said these words:

' Well, I guess I call you a cursed bad race of people, anyway, the whole tribe of you! And if Richard P. Hocking's got the sense in him, if it is in a year, if it is in ten years, to do anything to crush and swamp you out, he's just going to do it, and to that you may lay all there is of you !'

He sat again.

The manner of this huge man was impressive. At that moment he recalled a hundred-ton gun in action—a thing which does not often talk, but when it does, talks things that one cannot help hearing.

The captain of the *Huelva* looked at him, and was silent for a goodly number of the clock's ticks ; then he said:

' But that is talk. The question—do you consent or not to his Excellency's proposal?'

' I consent,' said Dick P. Hocking.

# CHAPTER IV.

## RUNNING THE BLOCKADE.

THE night came very gloomily. In those tropics it comes almost as suddenly as when one turns an electric button, and the red wires in the globes glower and die out rapidly into invisibility in the dark.

For two hours the sixteen boats of the *Huelva* and the *Montserrat* plied busily from one to the other, the ships being now only ten yards apart, the *Huelva* taking in a goodly mass of Sniders and Martinis, together with some uniforms, ammunition, flour, tins, and other stores. The process was slow, and before it was half over the *Huelva* ordered steam ahead.

They went forward, the smaller ship with her three lights, the *Huelva* in darkness. Cienfuegos was thirty miles to the north-west. Ten miles in advance of both went a smart picket-

boat, provided with signal-rockets, and steaming zigzag about the sea at the rate of twenty
knots.

At half-past seven it was as dark as the
gloomiest midnight—a quiet, stagnant night,
the sea heaving in flat, pale swells. At that
hour the picket-boat sent up a rocket. She
had sighted two steamer lights five or six miles
to the north-west—the two American ships-of-
war maintaining the blockade of Cienfuegos.

The *Montserrat* contained a thousand land
troops ; at once she and her convoy slackened
speed, and the rapid work of transhipment
began ; the picket-boat meantime panting back
to her parent ship, and both the American
cruisers, which had been loitering almost stationary with fires banked, starting in chase
toward the locality of the rocket.

By this time the captain of the *Montserrat*
had well digested his written instructions. He
was informed as to the exact spot of his next
destination, as to the spot at which he was to
rejoin the *Huelva*, as to the conditions under
which he was to keep the prisoner who would
be committed to his care. The most stringent
of these conditions was with regard to food.
Hocking must fast till the required sum in
specie was on board the *Montserrat*. It was

Appadacca's will—a will which no man had known to relent.

At this time Hocking had received notice of his transhipment. He had brought with him on board the *Huelva* a black handbag, and into this he had now packed the few things about him—some papers, a toothbrush, a pair of pyjamas. The bag was still not full. He threw it into a corner, and sat again on his hard stool, waiting.

Whether it was the cradling motion of the ship, or the state of hunger in which he lived, he was now in a chronic condition of drowsiness. He had hardly sat again when he began to nod.

But his slumber was of that light, spasmodic kind easily broken by disturbance. There stood an Admiral Colomb hand-lamp on a bracket in the room, giving a dim light ; and through his drowsing eyelids he seemed to see, as it were in dream, the single door of the apartment cautiously pushed back.

A figure entered the room. But it had all the characteristics of the figure of a dream, and for a moment or two, which seemed much longer, Dick P. Hocking really subconsciously believed that it *was* a dream-image.

It was a man rather below the middle height,

but with a figure erect and knit. He had about him a black cloak, the skirt of which trailed on the floor; over his forehead and nose was a black mask, but the pallid, chiselled, and hairless lips could be seen.

He must have paused, listening to Dick P. Hocking's breathing, for it was half a minute after the door moved before he entered; then he looked rapidly and, as it were, guiltily round, noticed the bag, stepped briskly and noiselessly toward it, pressed the clasp, and opened it.

At that moment Dick P. Hocking was wide awake. He started; he observed.

The man had a pile of something in his hands, which he was stuffing eagerly, with stealthy haste, into the bag; and Hocking saw what it was, and his avid nostrils smelled.

It was a quantity of bread cut in slices, and between the slices—meat. The whole was wrapped in two parcels of rice-paper; but as one parcel was being forced into the now full bag, the paper broke.

That gruff and rasping voice spoke. It said: 'Well, now——'

The visitor, or visitant, started, and at once turned to hurry away. Dick P. Hocking, in the passion of his gratitude, was up and after him.

HE STARTED BACK.

[*To face p.* 51.

Hocking just caught him by the mantle near the door. He said :

'No hurry, sonny. Just let Dick P. Hocking get your name and address down in this memorandum-book of his——'

Then he started backward. A stiletto, whose luminously-jewelled handle flashed like a galaxy even in the vague light, was at his breast. And as he started backward, the other man was gone.

Hocking, hungry as he was, sat again on his stool, and propped on his hand his meditative brow.

'Well,' he said, 'I'm *darned* if I don't call that handsome ! and handsomely done, too. "When thou doest thine alms, let not thy left hand know——"'

Then he said :

'But why in Jericho should the fellow be so mightily ashamed of feeding a hungry man? He *looked* ashamed, sure enough—or afraid, is it? Well, the world isn't done with Dick P. Hocking *yet*, sonny; and if ever he tumbles upon you again, it's settling off old scores between us we will be, I reckon——'

Beneath that gross front beat a heart strong in generous impulses as it was strong in rancour. He sat grumbling his thoughts of

4—2

future punishments and rewards ; but not for
long : in a few minutes the door opened again.
He clasped his bag hurriedly, and walked out
with it behind a lieutenant.

The last thought to enter his head was that
his visitor might be Appadacca himself—Appadacca, who, perhaps, had secretly relented ;
Appadacca, too sensitive to admit another being
into the knowledge of a weakness, too haughty
to confess before one of his crew even the
possibility of a change of purpose.

In ten minutes Hocking was on board the
*Montserrat*.  The two Spaniards steamed forward in the old direction.  The two Americans,
not eight knots away, came rapidly nearer.

Xagua Bay, at the head of which lies
Cienfuegos, now lay about north by west.  Its
entrance is only three miles wide ; the two
cruisers were therefore sufficient to maintain
an almost infallible blockade against ships of
equal or inferior speed.  Within the wider part
of the bay were mines and two masked batteries,
with which the Americans were under orders
to abstain from engaging ; but outside the
entrance the *Montserrat* ran the risk of almost
certain capture.

At the moment when the lights of the two
cruisers were judged to be four thousand yards

ahead, the *Montserrat* was commanded by trumpet-call to hide her lights. The *Huelva* was already in darkness.

Immediately one of the two cruisers hurried back toward the harbour entrance, to checkmate a dodge in the dark by the expected prize. Meanwhile, from each cruiser the beams of two electric searchlights streamed, peering in all directions over the sea.

But before it could be definitely determined by the cruiser which continued her southern course that there were not one, but two ships, with which she had to do, suddenly the three lights of the *Huelva* appeared in the darkness, and at the same time the *Huelva* swung round, and went steaming south ; the *Montserrat* steamed north-east ; and the cruiser followed in chase after the *Huelva*.

But it was like a chase between a greyhound and a bird. The officers of the cruiser, knowing the speed of the expected *Montserrat*, were endlessly mystified to observe the lights they pursued stealing rapidly from them, though their engines were toiling, with every aperture in the stokeholds closed, under forced draught.

On, however, they strained, two miles to southward, then in a wide curve, south by east, south-east, east, hopeless now of overtaking the fugitive thing already quite four miles ahead.

By this time the *Montserrat* had changed her north-easterly course to one north by west, and when about a mile from the harbour entrance, suddenly showed her lights ; the other cruiser waiting there promptly gave chase, and both went racing south-west, the cruiser gaining somewhat on the transport.

This manœuvre was adopted in order to draw away the cruiser from the harbour mouth, for at once the *Huelva*, which was about in the course of the transport and her pursuer, put out her lights ; and both cruisers a few minutes afterwards started in the wake of the *Montserrat.*

The chase now would have been short, and already the foremost of the cruisers was about to send a twelve-pounder across the sea, when once more the lights vanished, and instantly reappeared.

But the lights that reappeared were not the *Montserrat's.* The ship which the cruisers now chased was the *Huelva*, the transport calmly continuing her way south-west toward her next destination.

And now the great yacht, as it were, took the two cruisers in tow—led them dancing a mile or two in a southerly curve, and then came racing back due north. She passed through the harbour mouth while the cruisers were still two thousand yards to the south.

It was reported next day in all the newspapers of Europe and America that the *Montserrat* had run the blockade.

# CHAPTER V.

## SIXTY THOUSAND DOLLARS IN SPECIE.

THAT night, toward one, a small skiff put out from a creek grown to the water's edge with cocoanut-trees in a lonely part of Xagua Bay. She was rowed by a single negro, naked to the waist, and in her stern sat a man, wrapt in a voluminous coarse brown poncho, who left behind him as he moved a trail of the most delicious fragrance. He was smoking a green tobacco-leaf, moistened in cocoanut-water, and rolled before the first 'sickness' of the plant. It was the rebel leader, Gomez.

One of the points which, as the American-Spanish War developed itself, surprised and puzzled the world, was the inactivity of the insurgents on the island. Now that they had the great power of America on their side, important movements, brisk and energetic enterprises, were daily expected of them. But in vain was any such news awaited.

Gomez was a thick-set, powerful man, but with a surprising activity of movement. His face wore a continual expression of rough good-humour; but in the hard-headed look of his low, broad, slanting forehead was a suggestion of aggressive self-assurance.

The *Huelva* lay at anchor half a mile from the point of his embarkation; the land-troops had long since been disembarked from her, and a number of boats were even then making the last voyage shoreward with the remainder of her military freight.

Gomez swung himself nimbly up her side by the first end of rope he happened to catch. The captain of the *Huelva* awaited him. He was at once conducted aft, and into the regions of the cabin.

It was not the first time he had entered it; yet again he started with surprise, and a certain feeling of awe invaded a mind not very inclined to reverence. He was led through a complexity of corridors into a circular apartment, from whose dome hung a vague pink globe of softest light, making black the crimson hangings of Utrecht velvet in the semi-gloom, while the furnishing was of that heavy and rich pomp inaugurated by the Venetian noblesse of the fifteenth century. Gomez had sat down upon a swaying tabouret of silk and augite for some minutes, believing himself alone, when from the dimness of a far portion of the room there reached him a voice.

'Pray come nearer, Señor Gomez,' it said.

Gomez leapt up, Appadacca put down a book, and they were face to face.

'Well, I am glad you have been able to come after all, señor,' said Appadacca, 'though we meet under darker auspices this time than ever before. Our sport has ended in earnest, you see.'

'Sport, your Excellency? Señor, I call the holy Madonna to witness that this insurrection has never been sport to *me* ! Sport, say you? No sport to me, by the great God! Do you call, then, a hundred and fifty thousand starving women and children *sport* ?'

'No. The sport came first; the hundred and fifty thousand after. I always looked upon you as a person of excellent memory, Gomez.'

'Well, but, your Excellency, in the name of——'

'No. Pray calm yourself. I did not wish to see you in order to blame you for anything, but merely in order to guide you for the future. This absurd war is as much, perhaps, the fault of my own rather precipitate crew as it is your fault ; they know my private likes and dislikes, and foolishly imagine that they can fulfil my will by acting on their own whims.  You have heard of the catastrophe to an American warship in Havana Harbour——  However, it is of no importance.  But what you must now understand, Gomez, is that the hour is come for a total *volte face* on your side.  Your country is in genuine danger, my friend.'

'Cuba is my country, señor—not Spain.'

'Well, then, since you will have it so, I repeat, your country is in genuine danger.'

'Of what, señor ?'

'Of ceasing to be Spanish.'

'And of becoming Cuban, señor ?'

'No, of becoming—ha ! ha !—American.'

Gomez hung his head.

'The idea does not please you, Señor Gomez, I see.'

'I admit that it does not please me, señor.  But, by the Madonna, I do not know that I should not prefer to see Cuba a Yankee rather than a Spanish land.'

'Come, sir, do not lie to me in that fashion !' said Appadacca sternly.  'If your Mother is cruel, she is at least not disgusting ; if she lacerates your back, she at least does not revolt your stomach.  And you know it.  And in

your heart you prefer the cruel to the ugly
Mother. Nor is your memory really bad,
Gomez; nor have you *really* forgotten the
actual sequence of events—how that the
cruelties came after, not before, the provocation
which you and I, in our rôle of amateur in-
surrectionists, gave to them. This provocation,
sir, is what I have called our " sport "; and
since it has resulted in very serious earnest, I
say the time is now come for it to end.'

'Well, I have proceeded so far on your
Excellency's counsel and support. I suppose
that is what I must continue to do. But what
is it you propose, señor? Not that I should
disband any troops?'

' No; what are the plans of the Americans?'

' The first move which they intend, as far as
I understand it,' said Gomez, ' is to establish a
base in Cuba; and for that purpose they intend
to bombard the two forts at Matanzas on the
north coast in a day or two.'

' Then ?'

' Then a detachment of some five thousand
troops which are massing at Tampa, most of
them, I hear, inured against the yellow fever,
will be brought over.'

' Then will be your chance.'

' To turn against them, you mean, señor ?'

'I compliment your divination, Gomez.'

'But your Excellency must see that it is impossible to maintain an army without funds ; from these Yankees I await the sinews of war. And having once received their benefits, I am not the man to turn against them afterwards.'

'Then, do not receive their benefits.'

'But, señor——'

'No, I have foreseen your difficulty, Gomez. On the night of Thursday next, at eleven, the *Montserrat* will be at the Cape de Cruz, having on board the sixty thousand dollars in specie for which you telegraphed. The captain of the *Huelva* will give you instructions, as you pass up, under what conditions you are to receive the sum. Within another week you shall receive in addition several times that sum ; the condition being—loyalty, and, for the present, the cessation of the Sport.'

The two men continued to converse for yet an hour. Then Appadacca touched a button and rose ; Gomez was left to ponder drowsily over the interview, his senses being overpowered by an incense of myrrh which languidly fumed behind a drapery in the apartment.

At this time the *Montserrat* was moving

along the Isla de Pinos on her weather bow, steering east.

Avoiding the blockaded coast, she passed midway between Cape Catoche and the western-most point of Cuba, and then, steering north-west, made for the North Florida coast. By this time her name had been painted out, and the name *Caico* substituted.

Her whole object in the present cruise was to fulfil the obligation entered into with the *Huelva* to do Appadacca's bidding, in return for his assistance in taking her cargo and troops through the blockade.

Her captain had, therefore, no sort of animus against Dick P. Hocking ; and though stringently fulfilling his orders as to Hocking's diet, admitted him to a certain intimacy. Hocking was allowed to wander about the ship as he chose, and, meantime, with scrupulous economy, he subsisted on his rounds of meat and bread.

On the second night out, during the captain's watch, Hocking being then on deck, and the crescent moon shining in a brand of crushed silver over the smooth sea, the captain said :

' And as to the war, master, you bet on your own side, no doubt.'

' Well, I reckon I do,' said Dick P. Hocking,

'though there is precious little I know of it so far.'

'There is little to be known, señor. The Americans have blockaded the island yonder, and captured some few ships. But what they are thinking of in attacking ·Cuba, and leaving alone the weak point of Spain, is more than a man can know.'

'Which is the weak point of Spain?' asked Hocking, looking at the sky.

'Manila, surely,' answered the captain.

'Ah, how is that?' asked Hocking.

'Well, one may talk to you, being a prisoner, and so on. It is the thought of the Philippines that is troubling the big heads at Madrid—not Cuba. There are five warships at Manila, and —you would not believe it—they lack the common shot and shell and powder to do their work when an enemy puts in an appearance.'

'But forts—they've got forts, man, at the entrance to the harbour,' suggested Hocking musingly.

'Forts! The forts are much in the same way, as I happen to know. And if you knew how we Spaniards fall down before those islands! If harm came to them, there would likely be revolution and military dictatorship, and I know not what, as you'd see. Happily, you

Yankees are afraid of the forts, as you say, and daren't touch them yet.  By the time you begin to think of the matter, we'll be ready, don't you see ?'

'I do some.  But where have you run foul of these facts about the forts and ships, then ?'

'Oh, I !  I would know, you know.  I have been in the swim in high tides over yonder for the last three weeks on account of my cargo, and have heard the whispering one way and another.  Besides, am I not just back from the Eastern waters, where I took out troops to knock Alejandrino on the head ?'

'He another rebel ?' asked Hocking.

'Ay.'

'Rebels here in Cuba, and rebels yonder in the Philippines—it looks as if you were about wanting someone to lend a hand to your country some, these days, friend,' muttered Hocking.

'Ay, but it'll be a bad throw for those who try to lend the hand,' said the captain, with a nod of menace.

'H'm !  Well, we'll see into that, sonny,' mused Hocking.

The next evening the *Montserrat* put in at a deserted part of the Florida coast about seven miles north of Tampa Bay.

All that day Dick P. Hocking had been strangely studious, reading the 'Taçano' of Quevedo, a torn book of rather ancient Spanish which he found in the cabin. He could not understand two consecutive sentences. of it ; yet he seemed to pore with eagerness over the pages.

He had also found on a shelf in his cabin an old square bottle of small size, and in the bottom of this a little gum, some of it still liquid. This Dick P. Hocking had all the day in his pocket ; and there, too, lay a little pen-knife of fine amber as sharply-bladed as a razor.

He had now consumed the last of his sandwiches, and was again famishing.

At about seven o'clock, while the ship was coasting slowly, well in sight of land, the captain of the *Montserrat* entered his apartment. Hocking was studying, with glasses on nose, Quevedo's ' Taçano.'

' Now, señor,' said the captain, ' if you will write a note at my dictation—in Spanish, please—to your nearest agent for the amount, the boat is ready, and the first train from Tampa shall take my messenger.'

' I am ready,' said Hocking.

' One moment—I will bring you pen, ink, and paper.'

5

' Pencil will do,' said Hocking.

He took the slim brown pencil from the pocket of his note-book.

' Bring us a sheet of paper, capitan.   Or stay —this will do—this will do.'

In a moment he had torn the fly-leaf from the ' Taçano.'   On one side it was yellow, on the other white.

At the bottom of the white side were three lines of print which the captain, bending over Hocking as he wrote, saw without seeing, noticed without noticing.   It looked like some announcement of the publisher of the book.

Had the printed words been Spanish, their meaning would probably have entered in a mechanical, unconscious way into his pre-occupied brain.   But they were English.   His eyes rested long upon them, and did not see them.   They were so obviously natural just where they were.

Hocking scribbled in pencil :

' DEAR SIR,

' You will be good enough to deliver to the bearer of this, *without delay*, sixty thousand dollars for my account in gold specie of the United States.   I have strong personal reasons for writing in Spanish, and for approaching you

in this manner.    See below—my signature.
The matter is very urgent.
' Yours truly,
' RICHARD P. HOCKING.

' To JAMES M. SHERMAN,
' Halifax, Georgia.'

And as the captain turned to procure an
envelope, Dick P. Hocking said to himself :
' I'm darned if it doesn't look like getting
there !'
The words printed at the bottom of the leaf
were these :

' Tell Gov. Span. ship near Tam. going south
at once.    I pris.    Give money, but capture.'

At about seven two men, able to speak
good English, were landed on the coast.    They
walked to Tampa, and within an hour took train
northward, bearing Hocking's pencilled and
printed messages.
Few as were the words printed, they were
yet a model of the man's measureless patience,
his minute acuteness—that patience and that
cuteness which had gone to the amassing of
his uncounted millions.    Upon the cutting-out
of those few letters from the thin - leaved
book, and the pasting them together in the

5—2

required order, he had spent fifteen hours, working with thick, buxom, blunt fingers never intended for that sort of labour. He had known well that the least flaw, the slant of a letter, the trace of a joining, and attention would be attracted. And in the end there was not, as a matter of fact, the least flaw, or slant, or trace of joining. Over the whole, when the work was done, he might have scribbled the word 'Thorough.'

By noon of the next day the two messengers were back at Tampa, and their walk slanted to the right under the weight of the cash-boxes which they carried.

At two the *Montserrat* stood away to the south by east, bound for her rendezvous with the *Huelva.*

At half-past three she sighted a long bolster of brownish smoke on the southern horizon.

Fearing trouble, she pricked off her course east, and put her last two knots upon her speed ; but in doing so, she too poured out a goodly volume of dark redundant smoke.

The day was bright and hot, the sea glassy. The two ships were ten miles apart.

Dick P. Hocking stood near a taffrail astern, looking over the glistening expanse of pale water. He was as content as a man could be ;

his fists bulged out his lax voluminous pockets, and rattled the few pieces of coin within them ; his squat right leg cocked out ; between his lips was one of the most aromatic cigars or Havana ; he had just been learning what a joy it is to eat. The *Montserrat* seemed a little kingdom, and he its king.

He watched that growing bolster of smoke ; but he could stand beans both ways—good luck as well as bad. His face showed no exultation. He did not forget that he was smoking an exceptional cigar.

The chase intensified to straining-point, but it was hopeless for the trooper. Her highest speed was nineteen knots, and there came tearing after her a thing all guns and tubes and gleaming mechanism, at the rate of twenty-three an hour. It was the gunboat *Terror*.

A quarter of an hour before sunset—that is to say, within two hours from the start—the *Terror* was two miles away on the port quarter of the *Montserrat*, and it was then that a puff of smoke was seen to issue from the warship's beam ; a half-minute afterwards a gross hoot of sound ; and Dick P. Hocking looked upward to see a raging baleful thing fly quarrelling with itself over his head, to plunge into the sea two hundred yards away in a mêlée of flame and spouting foam.

He nodded his head.

'Capitan mio!' he said, 'this time I guess-——'

The *Montserrat* was now a flurry of pale-faced men scurrying wildly about, but she continued her course till, five minutes later, a thing rushed past her bowsprit, carrying it along with it, and immediately her captain was seen at the mainmost shrouds, hurriedly hauling down something. The beat of her engines slackened ; the *Terror* grew large and near ; there were boats in the water, and soon a young lieutenant was bowing before Dick P. Hocking.

Hocking was, as it proved, in a considerable hurry to get his feet once more on United States soil. Even while a prize-crew was being got on board the *Montserrat*, he was on board the *Terror*, and with him the cash-boxes.

He arrived at Tampa in the early evening, and at once set off northward. He had several things to get off his chest.

The first was to announce that the ship known as the *Huelva*, a craft passing for a monstrous yacht, but in reality possessing the arms and armature of a ship-of-war, would very likely be lying in wait between Cuba and

Key West for the next transport-ship to Havana.

Also, there was not a member of the Naval Committee in whose mind the name of Dick P. Hocking was not of high significance. And to each, in the week that followed, Dick P. Hocking made a point of mentioning one word —the word ' Manila.' And that word he impressed upon them all, and told them why. A week later the Stars and Stripes waved over the town.

He had all his life been a busy man, but he had never been in such a heat of business as now in his life before.

He had to send advices in urgent haste to a host of correspondents ; certain bills drawn upon them by him at certain dates were invalid, and must be dishonoured ; but he found that some of them had already been discharged in favour of the house of Campos.

Also, Hocking in these days was very much in the company of naval experts and builders, and the man's whole mind seemed open to drink in the details of an entire new science. At an interview with the manager of Cramp of Philadelphia, he said :

' And now, how long to build ?—for that, I guess, is about the main question.'

'A battleship, in general—two years.'

'Ah, but we are not discussing battleships at the present. Let us confine ourselves to torpedo-boats. Seems to me they are about what the future's got to reckon with.'

'Well, of course that varies, according to the orders a firm has on hand. Nine months—six months.'

'Six months. Now, I put to you a question in simple proportion. Suppose it takes two hundred men six months to build a torpedo-boat, how long will it take four hundred men?'

'Something in the neighbourhood of three months, I should guess, sir.'

'That's about it, I reckon,' said Hocking. 'And how long would it take eight hundred men, if your brain doesn't break down under the strain?'

The manager laughed.

'Well, Mr. Thompson,' said Hocking, 'there is one thing I want to impress strongly upon you, if we do business together—and just see you don't be forgetting it, neither—that I am one of the richest men on the face of this globe.'

# CHAPTER VI.

## A SPANIARD THINKS.

THE *Huelva* passed out of Xagua Bay soon
after darkness fell, not even careful to mask
her lights. There was a short chase by the two
blockading cruisers towards the south-west, and
a blank shell splashed into the sea a hundred
feet astern of her. But she ran on her way as
unconcernedly as a high-geared bicycle chased
by a stout policeman.

At the moment news was scarce and rare.
It was said at Cienfuegos that an invasion of
Cuba was impending by an American army of
some 20,000 regulars and 50,000 volunteers;
it was said that Admiral Dewey had set out
with his Far Eastern fleet from Mirs Bay, with
Manila as his objective—nothing more. Meantime, as the captain of the *Montserrat* had
informed the captain of the *Huelva*, an easy
prize for the latter was about to sail from Key

West with a valuable military cargo, stores, and specie for Havana; and when the captain communicated this news by telephone to Appadacca, and asked if he should prosecute a capture, Appadacca replied: 'You may.'

And so it was that the *Huelva*, with close on two thousand tons of coal in her bunkers, steered west, and next morning was making her way leisurely at twenty knots off Cape S. Antonio, the western extremity of Cuba.

Immanuel Appadacca had just cast himself upon a couch, and there lay back, musing. It was in his library, where all night he had been poring over a volume of old-Arab verse-lore. Here no hint of the day intruded, but tongues of blue and green flame, writhing from open-work censers of Etruscan pottery, diffused a species of tinted half-light. The long piles of books were mostly hidden by tapestries of Arras.

He was roused from his thoughts by a sound in a neighbouring alcove—a whistle. He rose and went to the tube. A voice said:

'There is a large barque on our port bow—has hoisted the Union Jack. She is close-hauled on the starboard tack, wanting to weather the Cape. Shall I——'

'Make her lie to,' said Appadacca. 'Do not harm her; get news.'

The *Huelva* turned her course across the bows of the barque, sent a three-pounder over the sea, and in a few minutes slackened speed sufficiently to get a pinnace out. The barque lay to at her signal.

The first lieutenant took with him one of the crew of the main-deck four-inch guns, a London lad called Roach. And from Roach's interpreting it was learnt that the barque was from Liverpool, bound to Belize with iron sleepers, and had met near the Florida Reef an American transport, convoyed by a cruiser and two gun-boats, bound for Havana. By one of the gun-boats she had been bespoken, and had learned—news.

The transport was at once guessed by the *Huelva's* captain to be the one which the *Huelva* was seeking. (She was being convoyed in consequence of the warning of Dick P. Hocking.)

Within half an hour Appadacca in his library had in his hand a despatch giving this and the other items of news gathered from the barque.

The chief of these related to the event at Manila.

Eleven Spanish ships, armed with old muzzle-loading guns incapable of destroying a sea-fowl at three thousand yards, had stood still to be shelled by exquisitely modern long-range rifled cannon in Manila harbour; old sandbag forts had spluttered ineffectually at the invading fleet through impossible old brass guns. Manila, whose very name was poetry, was at the mercy of a Yankee commodore.

The Spaniards had not killed one single American. They were reported to have injured not one single ship. Some of the shells which they had fired had struck, but they had been blank; they had ricocheted, and harmlessly fallen into the sea. Why, being at long distance with bad guns, and so at a disadvantage, they had not adopted the very elementary tactical manœuvre of coming to close quarters, was not explained. They had died heroically under a perfect tempest of shrapnel, and had done nothing.

And this was at Manila, the land of aromas, the nosegay of ancient Spain, whose name was poetry!

It was a place very dear to the Spaniard. Immanuel Appadacca thought of it as the future domain of Dick P. Hocking, and smiled. Among the nutmegs soon would clank and throb a red-brick factory; through the groves of almond and cornel would scream and rattle the cars of an elevated railroad—I guess.

He smiled. Then, suddenly, he crumpled the paper in his clenched fist, and cast himself face downward on a divan, heaped with llama wools ; over his face pressed his small jewelled hands, and through his body passed the slightest spasmodic movements.

He was a man of the acutest mental calibre. He could knit his brows and see far into a fact where many another, even with the aid of glasses, would find only darkness. And as he lay, quivering slightly, he peered deeply into Destiny, with travailing, anguished brain.

Already, from that beginning, he seemed to see the end.

That beauty which he loved, was it not the hectic beauty of the consumptive patient — doomed, doomed ?

Or was it not like the beauty of woman, weak, skin-deep, spoiling at the first rough blast, the first unsparing sun ; unfit to combat and survive the rude, earnest traffic of the coming centuries ?

The Latin races—were they then doomed to go, to pass for ever away ?

And leave what behind ? Nothing but one vast workshop, side by side with one vast Stock Exchange, and one vast railway-station ? Here was a survival of the unfittest! So it seemed to him.

But, at least, the old beautiful was worth

fighting for, and dying for, as against the new ugly. And there was at any rate one man prepared to fight and die for it—the name of him, Immanuel Appadacca.

He lay there contending with a thought which rose in his brain. It was a tremendous thought; he was unwilling to give it entertainment, but it persisted, he struggled, and it came back and conquered him.

He leapt up, he touched an electric button, and instantly a dark-skinned man in Moorish robes was bowing before him.

'You are to see, Ali,' said Appadacca, 'whether the holy Father can find it convenient to grant me an audience here within the hour.'

The Moor, making an obeisance, retired backwards.

Appadacca reseated himself, took up the book he had been perusing, and again began to read. In twenty minutes the arras at an angle of the apartment opened, and a tall man of austere and pallid countenance stood there.

His face was very long and thin, and darkened over lip and jaws and chin with an inky indication of shaven hair; the black eyes rather too close together, and downward-looking, and shifting; the forehead narrow, high, and bald at the

corners ; the chin very prominent. An odour
of peace was about him.

A silver crucifix hung on his breast, a rosary
at his hip ; his lank form was closely wrapped
by a surtout, banded at the waist.

Appadacca rose and bowed. And he said :

' Holy Father . . .'

The priest inclined his head, and his lips
muttered :

' My son . . .'

# CHAPTER VII.

## SAXON v. LATIN.

THE two men sat near together. The priest, with his long left forefinger stroked gently down and down the smooth part of his crucifix with a slow, clandestine movement. Appadacca had thrown himself into a violet velvet arm-chair with an appearance of carelessness, yet, in doing so, had slightly shifted its position, so that his own face could not readily be seen, while a pallid greenish ray from one of the lamps shone full upon the priest's wan countenance.

Appadacca said :

' I have news, Father Pedro. Manila is in the hands of the Americans.'

' Soh, my son.'

' You know ?'

' Yes. I had Sancho with me in the chapel,

surmising that something had been heard.   He
told me all.'

'But the details—they are interesting.'

'Ah ?'

'Eleven Spanish ships have been destroyed
—burnt, sunk, or battered.   No American has
been killed ; it appears that no American ship
has been seriously injured.'

'That is so,' said Father Pedro, with no
sign of emotion, only his downward-looking
eyes continually moved, and his finger lightly
stroked the crucifix.   He waited.   He knew
well that he had not been summoned to a conference with Immanuel Appadacca for nothing.

'Yet the sailors who fought on our side
fought bravely—one, it seems, might almost say
heroically,' proceeded Appadacca.

'They were Spaniards,' said Father Pedro.

'Yet they effected nothing.'

'It is strange.'

'Hardly strange, perhaps.   The inference as
to cause is obvious.'

'What, then, is your inference, my son ?'

'That they were badly generaled.'

'It is an inference, certainly.'

'The old story, Father, you will say.'

'Ah, perhaps those words might possibly rise
to the lips.'

' Badly generaled—badly generaled in Cortes and on battlefield, in council-chamber and at sea. And badly, because selfishly.'

' Do not suppose that my silence means dis-agreement,' said Father Pedro after half a minute.

' Quite so. I say selfishly. But the selfish-ness will persist to the end : that, assuredly, will be the last thing to die in Spain. Our prominent men seek to be more prominent, and Spain is the victim. The people are devoted ; the devotion of their great men is corrupted by the taste of power. And if that persists—and it will—we shall lose ; we are doomed.'

' I follow you carefully,' said Father Pedro.

' A man, however,' said Appadacca—and his face was not visible—' who was as prominent as possible could not seek to be more pro-minent.'

' No ; that is so—that is certainly so,' assented the priest.

' And the inference you draw, Father Pedro?'

' Tell me your whole mind, and I will tell you plainly if I am in accord,' said the Jesuit.

Appadacca threw down a book.

' A military dictator would be such a man as I have described.'

'Certainly; such a thought cannot fail to occur to one.'

'You agree, then?'

'In the main.'

'But the consequence would be large, Father Pedro.'

'Large, certainly,' said the priest, and a smile flitted over his lips; 'highly important for Spain, at least.'

'But I do not see why we should not be quite candid with each other—I mean *larger* than that.'

'My son, my son——' said the priest.

'The holy Father disapproves. For the present I will say no more.'

Appadacca's lips closed tightly. Both men were cunning. Appadacca had the human instinct to seek ghostly fellowship with, and consent to, a thought which something within him warned him was monstrous. The priest now divined the thought, and adored it, and wished to conceal his adoration of it; and Appadacca was half doubtful, half divining of the priest's adoration, and wished to force an avowal of his approval.

'I have not expressed disapproval of anything, my son,' said Father Pedro. 'Of what should I disapprove? What, then, are those *larger* consequences of a dictatorship in Spain to which you refer ?'

Appadacca picked up a book, opened it, and, looking steadily at the priest, said :

' The greatest war which has yet occurred in history.'

The padre perceptibly started, and his finger paused midway in its descent down the length of the crucifix.

' May the Immaculate preserve our hands from the stain of blood !' he said.

Appadacca's lip slightly curled.

' They are already stained, Father,' he said—'all our hands. The whole present world is in a state of bloody-minded enmity. Is it not written that he that hateth his brother is a murderer ? The nations, I think, have been slow to adopt the Christian Idea. They were never so very, very far removed from it as at this hour. The stain of blood, you say ? Our hands are thick with it, Father Pedro !'

' That is in spite of the Church, my son. But you speak of great matters. For what reasons, think you, must a military dictatorship in Spain be followed by the awful thing of which you speak ?'

The padre was a man intimately familiar with the inner minutiæ of European affairs, and their sequences one upon another; he knew well the answer to the question which he asked, but he asked it for reasons of his own in reference to Appadacca.

Appadacca said :

' Holy Father, you are aware that the world is at present in the hands of two chief races— the Latin and the Teutonic. There is a third power, the Empire of Russia, which is neither, being Slav ; but this power is so much in sympathy, both from its innate affinities and from the force of circumstances, with the Latin, that we may class it roughly with the Latins. French, Spanish, Italians, Russians—British, Germans, Austrians, Americans : there, for the most part, are the two *primâ facie* camps. I say *primâ facie ;* for, in reality, between all those in the second camp who live together with those in the first camp on one mainland there is an affinity, and a resemblance, and a sympathy, which, in a general war, will not fail somehow to show itself. Did I tell you that at Cienfuegos I received a telegram from Cadiz informing me that the crew of the German cruiser *Oldenburg* went ashore there, and fraternized enthusiastically with the men of our *Pelayo?* The sailors of the two ships marched through the streets arm in arm, wearing one another's caps. Now, American and German must be bracketed together in respect to race; yet we find German sailors wearing the caps of Spanish sailors at a time when Spanish and American are at war, the fact being that the Germans have now become very much more like the unrelated Spaniards at their doors than like the related Americans far away. Our barque this morning also gives us the news that four German warships are hasting toward Manila with some unknown object, certainly not friendly to America. I have a purpose in saying all this, if you will bear with me.'

' You interest me profoundly, my son.'

'Well, then,' said Appadacca, 'from our second race-camp we must take, for the practical purpose of computing the sympathy on our side in this war, both the German and the Austrian. And you have left two lonely nations, both disconnected with the communism of nations on the Continent of Europe—two only—Britain and America.'

Appadacca paused. The padre drew a deep breath.

' These two nations,' continued Appadacca, ' are, in reality, very unlike each other. There can be no radical sympathy between them :

they are too far apart in every respect.
America, to a cultured mind, is as much more
repulsive than England, as England is less
beautiful than the Venice of the Doges ; but,
unlike each other as they are, they are more
like each other than either is like any of the
Continental nations, and sympathy depends
upon similarity.   In a game of universal war,
where each chooses his own partner, these two
would assuredly fight together : it would be a
Saxon League.'

' A formidable combination, my son.'

'Yes ; and possibly it might be made still
more so, by becoming, not a Saxon, but a
Teuton League—sympathy of blood proving
stronger than sympathy of manners, and
Germany, Austria, Sweden, and the like,
joining with their cousins.   On the other side
would be France and Russia, Spain and Italy.'

' But that is heterodox,' said the padre, with
the gleam of a laugh in his eyes.   ' Italy goes
with the Teutons—with Germany, with Austria.'

Appadacca smiled.

' You and I know differently, Father ; the
rulers of Italy, perhaps—not Italy.   The Triple
Alliance is dying ; a telegram from the *Huelva*
to a certain village in Calabria would, as you are
aware, kill it.   The first object of an Italian revo-

lution would be the reduction of the cost of
the standing army ; and with this reduction, or
even with the demand for it, the Alliance would
be at an end.    And it is not far off—probably
not a year away.    Italians are now paying
more than 50 per cent. of all incomes in taxes.
How and by whom all that could be swiftly
swept away, you and I know.    It was not
precisely for this buffoonery of government
that Mazzini, Cavour, Garibaldi, and Victor
Emmanuel gave their lives.'

'Your Latin races, my son, make excellent
soldiers, but bad generals.    They are all badly
led, to come back to the old point.'

'Precisely.    Their general shall be—Russia.'

'You say "*shall* be"?'

'That is, if a military dictatorship happens
to be set up in Spain.'

'Who would be the dictator—Weyler?'

'He is a brute!'

'Polavieja?'

'He is not disinterested.'

'Then Martinez Campos?'

'He would be my choice.'

'And your choice would infallibly succeed?'

'Yes.    Their great need is money.    My
choice would be abundantly supplied with
money.'

'Are you still very rich, my son?'

'Yes: I possess the *Huelva* and her crew.'

'But why not call the dictator Appadacca?'

'I see you consent to the general scheme, Father.'

'Ah! to discuss is not invariably to approve. But why not call the dictator Appadacca?'

'No, Father Pedro. That is not precisely in my way; your inner instincts do not admit it as suitable to my personality. With your help, I prefer to direct from the dark.'

'Direct what?'

'The apparent anarchy that must ensue during the process of revolution both in Spain and Italy. In Spain there will follow repudiation of the National Debt. And you are aware who will be principally interested in that matter.'

'France and Russia——'

'France will claim Ceuta, face to face with Gibraltar; Russia will claim Minorca—at least, it will be persistently suggested to her to do so; nor will the persistence be very necessary, I think. England will protest, and flame. The naval bases of Spain in European waters are the envy, and are destined to become the apples of discord, of the races, to range them in final fight for the possession and government of the earth.'

'I follow you,' said Father Pedro. 'But to state a scheme such as that which you have in mind, and to claim for it the sanction of the Church, whose robes are Peace, and whose tabernacle is Compassion, are two different matters, my son.'

'The Church in your person disapproves, Father?' asked Appadacca insinuatingly, his eyes musing on the priest's face.

'My son, yes.'

'Ah, then, I, for my part, find the sole responsibility onerous; I drop the notion. I thought that perhaps the tacit support of the Vatican, obtained through your great influence, might, in Spain, help forward the initial steps, but—I admit my error.'

The priest blinked. He was a man of intense passions on national questions; he felt that he had said too much, and not enough.

'The end you propose is, nevertheless, blessed, my son,' he said, looking low under his eyes. 'As I understand it, it is the providing of a good soldier with a good general ; it is the salvation of Spain.'

'And the aggrandizement,' added Appadacca eagerly. 'It is Morocco, South America, Mexico, and the West Indies, spreading the actual Spain of to-day over the world.'

' I repeat, it is a blessed end.'

' Yet the Church rejects it !'

' Striving to be harmless as doves.'

'And forgetting to be wise as serpents.'

' Have no fear ; She is that too—that too.'

' The Latin League of which I have spoken is purely Catholic, Father, and Græco-Catholic.'

' I am vividly alive to it.'

'And the end here, if anywhere, should justify the means.'

The padre smiled.

'Ah! I am reassured,' said Appadacca. 'The Church, come now, is a consenting maiden, using sweet, reluctant, amorous delays. I dare say that you are at one with me.'

The priest stood up, with fixed lips.

' But,' he said, ' make haste! and when you strike, strike home.'

# CHAPTER VIII.

## THE PHANTOM FLEET.

Now, it happened that one of Dick P. Hocking's chosen satellites was a certain Rev. Silas M. Petersen, of the Methodist Free Church, whose Brooklyn chapel Dick P. Hocking had built ; and the Rev. Petersen was often to be found in the company of Hocking, in Fifth Avenue, for he possessed unction, freedom of speech, and a shrewd, practical head of the world—things dear to the cockles of Dick P. Hocking's heart, I guess. So Hocking patronized and sheltered the parson under the warmth of his mighty arm, and the parson lived there as in a pleasant greenhouse of comfort, liking the patronage ; 'for,' said he, ' talk as you like, I guess you can't get along without it, any way.'

Now, about the time when the priest and Appadacca were fencing in the cabin of the

*Huelva*, these two others were travelling south alone in a Pullman car, with Hampton Roads in the eye of purpose, where the *Union*, recalled by telegram from Carracas, awaited them. Dick P. Hocking was taking the Rev. Silas M. Petersen with him on an exciting cruise.

And as they sped along Petersen put his elbow on his knee, and, in the midst of a conversation, said:

' Now, I'll tell you, sir, how these same Latin races, as we name them, strike me——'

Hocking nodded, and leant forward to listen. Petersen, though of goodly proportions, was a very small edition of Hocking, but uglier in figure and face, his legs being very short and his body long, so that he had rather the look of a pig standing on its hindquarters. Over his fat yellow cheek and upper lip a few hairs, which one might count, straggled and curled. His nose turned up, and his thin, falsetto voice spoke all in oily coils and modulations. He leered always downwards and far sidewards when he spoke to one.

Often from those fleshy lips came words wonderfully related to the facts of a matter.

' Well, let us have it,' said Hocking.

' Isn't it just about like this somehow,' said Petersen: ' that just as each separate country grows its men and its women, so the whole earth, as a whole, grows its men and its women ; only the men and the women of the whole earth, as a whole, are not individuals, but nations ?'

Dick P. Hocking, looking at the carpet, nodded slowly several times.

'Well, now, it's about striking me,' proceeded Petersen, 'that this same Latin race is just what we may name the Woman of the civilized world. They have the pretty ways, the weakness, the excitability, the cleverness, and, I guess, the sharp nails of woman. They can't kill, but they can get in a good scratch at a man's eyes—till you subdue them, and train them to fetch your slippers, and darn your socks. And we others are the Man—we Americans, those Britishers—we have about got the enterprise, the independence, and the world-care of the man. And I put this question to you, sir : What is the natural end to a man and a woman brought into daily close relations ?'

Dick P. Hocking looked sharply up with a kind of glad surprise, a light in his eyes, and stretching out his arm, he shouted :

' *Marriage !*'

'That's about what it comes to, I guess,' said Petersen—'marriage ; and till that marriage comes off in the cathedral of the world, with the angels for bridesmaids, and all the fiddles of God a-playing and making merry, neither that man nor that woman is going to have any idea of what true happiness is about like.'

'Well I'm darned!' cried Dick P. Hocking, with waving arm—'well, if I'm not darned! Why, that's the very selfsame notion, man, that's been hovering round the back of my brain for the last two weeks—only I didn't know how to say it to myself!'

'That's so,' answered Petersen. 'Only the Woman still has to be fought for, and won. There's going to be some blood spilt over that business, I reckon. She will have to be conquered before she will give in. She's a maid, I guess, used to her freedom, loath to part with her habit of virginity—and her nails are sharp. She will have to be cruelly banged and bastinadoed before she comes round to reason, and then she will love the man for conquering her, and she will be all voluntary service, and tender cares, and she will be mending his things, and be making him smart and handsome like herself, and *he* will be making her healthy, and matronly, and content, and the mother of the world. That's Marriage.'

'Look here, my son,' said Dick P. Hocking, 'how about that new schoolhouse of yours?

Not roofed yet ?    Just do me the favour to put
me down for another thousand dollars on your
list !    It's the very thing I've been thinking all
the time !    And that's just about how we'll
have to work it, or else Dick P. Hocking is
a fool, and so is Silas M. Petersen ! and that's
a lie, whoever says it.'

But now the warning change of sound when
a train slows into a station was heard ; and
early the next morning the *Union* was out of
sight of land, steering south-east by east toward
the east Cuban coast.

Toward night she fell in, north of the small
islands called Cayo Romano, with the American
squadron, consisting of the battleships *Iowa*
and *Indiana*, the armoured cruiser *New York*,
and four gunboats taken from the patrol
squadron.    They were steaming eastward, bent
upon the discovery of the Spanish squadron
which had lately left Cape Verde Islands, in
order, it was not doubted, to cross the Atlantic.

It was with a view to this Spanish squadron
that Hocking himself was now promenading
the seas.    The speed of the *Union* was con-
siderably higher than the average of the
American squadron.    He would serve as a
scout, and he would see a battle.

The next day it was heard at Washington

that the Spanish ships, consisting of four
armoured cruisers and three destroyers, the
flagship being the *Infanta Maria Theresa*, had
been sighted off Barbadoes ; and this news
the *Union* learned at Porto Plate, in northern
St. Domingo.

With all her speed she went on eastward.

Meantime, with the certainty of an engagement now in their minds, the Washington
Government hurriedly despatched the battleships *Massachusetts* and *Texas* and the armoured
cruiser *Brooklyn* to reinforce the rather deficient
American squadron. These three, however,
were now a long way behind, needing three or
four days to come up with the main body.

These were sighted in the longitude of Andros
Island by the *Huelva ;* and at the next noon
the main body of the squadron was passed by
her on the starboard bow. She was then
tearing furiously eastward, having now learnt
the news of the advance of the Spanish
fleet to meet the American, about to be rein-
forced as the latter was. Appadacca had no
intention that a fresh Spanish squadron should
be annihilated by a superior force at that
moment : he had other views.

Meantime, the *Union*, with Dick P. Hocking
and his militant spiritual prompter, was heading

7

briskly along the south Porto Rico coast.
Then, changing her course somewhat to the east
of south, steamed so for half a day, when, an
hour before sunset, the look-out man in the
top sighted the advancing Spanish fleet.   Their
torpedo-destroyers were, of course, of consider-
ably higher speed than the *Union*, and as soon
as their number and disposition had been made
out, the *Union* turned tail, and went hasting
back   northward,   hoping   to   encounter   the
advance force of the American squadron not
later than three the next day somewhere in the
longitude of 70, and report.

The night was very dark, and when the day
was coming, a dense and dank sea-born haze,
white but impenetrable, muffled and blanketed
all the ocean and the ship in a mystery of
moisture.

But almost instantaneously, as the first
horizontal beam of the sun shot in intense
radiance over the sea-surface, the mist thinned
and vanished into clear, hot day ; and at this
sudden transformation - scene, the first thing
which the Rev. Petersen, in his morning mufti
at an aft-taffrail, and with him the watch on
deck of the *Union*, perceived, was a huge ship,
seeming to walk the water with the gliding
buoyancy of a sea-gull wetting alternate wing-

tips in the brine—a ship not a mile from them, bearing down straight upon them.

At her main she flew a flag orange in colour, and bearing in the centre a device in black, altogether unknown to any published code in the world. It was the *Huelva*.

# CHAPTER IX.

## CABLE CUTTING.

ALL the details of the swiftly-advancing ship became terribly distinct to the crew of the *Union* as the pure-white smoke of the fog suddenly thinned and dispersed.

She was three-masted, the fore-mast being much the tallest of the three, with a long space between it and the mizzen-mast, sufficient to admit four tall funnels, from the hindermost of which now swayed upwards a languid streak of smoke. At the first glance the eye detected that she was armed, but though she had no visible ram, there seemed a good difference of length between her upper deck and her water-line ; and about her bows, her beam, the lithe sheer and under-curves of her stern, there was a delightful suggestion of clipping levity and grace, which imparted to her the air of some winged sea-horse. Under plain sail and courses, without the aid of steam, she could flit with all that weight through eleven knots.

The Rev. Silas M. Petersen hurried below. Dick P. Hocking was still asleep in his bed. Petersen broke into his room and shook him.

'There's a large ship ripping straight down upon us,' he said; 'it strikes me the meaning of her is trouble. I reckon it is the—the *Huelva!*'

Dick P. Hocking lifted his body; his heavy-lidded eyes were puffed with sleep.

'What's her painting?' he said.

'A bluey white.'

'Then it's she.'

He heaved himself from the bed. As he did so, he heard running feet above, and a single bark of cannon.

'Well, it looks as if they'd got me again this time,' said Hocking.

'If we haven't got them,' answered Petersen.

'What's your point?' said Hocking.

'What about those twenty-five Winchesters?' answered Petersen.

Down upon Petersen's back came Dick P. Hocking's mighty paw with a slap.

'You are the little parson for me!' he cried.

'What *you* have got to do is to *hide*,' said Petersen.

'That's it, I reckon. But where?'

'Why, here.   And that great chest, there, it's about made to take those Winchesters.'

At this moment down rushed the *Union's* captain.

'You have heard, sir?' he cried breathlessly. 'It is that Spanish privateer we met at La Guayra.   Do we yield?   There is still five minutes' running.'

'Yield, yield,' said Hocking.   'I am not at home—that's about all you need remember for the time being.   There are twenty-five brand-new Winchester rifles on board this ship; just order a couple of hands to get them into this chest before those beastly pirates get there. And don't forget ammunition and a good hundred and fifty rounds of shot.   And look you, captain, here is the little man whose orders have got to go during my temporary absence. I guess he's about right for both worlds, and you remember it.'

He pointed to Petersen.   And deliberately he lifted himself into the bed again, put out his arm, took a cigar and lit it, drew the bedclothes to his chin, and lay there calm and huge as a fallen monolith of Stonehenge.

By this time the slowing engines of the *Union* were calling out in two tones long-drawn

whines of melancholy rest after dire labour;
then, where travail and complex turmoil had
been, was perfect quiet. The ship lay stationary
on the gently heaving water. Three boats were
being lowered from the *Huelva*, which was
now forging slowly through a twenty-point
curve.

The Rev. Silas M. Petersen was saying to
two men on the poop of the *Union*:

'That ship, you may be certain, is in a hurry
to get somewhere. I'll swear—though swear-
ing isn't precisely in my line of business—that
she was at full speed when I first sighted her.
I guess what she wants to do is to get at the
Spanish fleet the first moment she can. Even
if she sends a prize-crew aboard here, she
doesn't mean to wait for them; we can't keep
pace with her. The moment we see the last
sign of her smoke, captain, it isn't in our
pockets we'll be resting our hands.'

The little fleet of three boats came nearer.
The *Union* put out her trellis-work escalier,
the eager mixture of tongues in the boats
reached her, and in a minute men were hurrying up the steps.

One man, a Catalan giant, with a red
bandana tied tight concealing his head from
the eyebrows to the neck behind, came

up to Petersen, who wore the parson's collar
and a short jacket.   The collar perhaps attracted
him.   He said in rough, broken English :

' You give our ship ?'

' We yield,' answered Petersen.

'What you got here ?'

' Nothing.   Ballast, and may be a thousand
dollars or so in money, and stores.'

' Ah, we go to see.   You come too.'

The twenty-five who had come on board
then scattered to ransack the ship, with the
exception of one, who bore in his hand a large
official-sized envelope apparently full of papers.
Petersen, the captain, and the first officer
descended to the cabin with the Catalan, to
whom they had handed a bunch of keys, the
register, and the clearance ; with them also
went a negro and two Creoles from the
*Huelva*.

Dick P. Hocking's door was in a partition
jalousied in the upper portion, plain varnished
walnut below.   It was one of a series of doors on
both sides of the passage ; all were closed, most
unlocked.   Only Hocking's was locked, and
two others of which Petersen had taken the
precaution to turn the key.   Three locked
doors, he reasoned, would be less an object of
curiosity than one.

When the Catalan came to the first locked door, he found in his bunch no key to fit it.

' The key to this port,' he said.

Where was it?

The captain was not sure, Petersen was not sure; someone ran to look; but it was weary waiting, and the Catalan appeared in a desperate hurry. At last the key was found; the door was opened; there was nothing worth seeing in the room.

Then came the second locked door. Where was the key? It was not to be found. Three *Union* men ran to look, and there was more waiting. It was only after the Catalan had flung his hand and said : ' Oh, afterwards I will come to look,' that someone came running with the key. The door was opened; there was nothing worth seeing in the room.

They came to the door behind which lay Hocking. The key could not be found. Again the Catalan flung his hand.

' I cannot wait,' he said ; 'afterwards.'

They passed on, searching. They were interrupted by a trumpet-call from the *Huelva ;* there was no time, the boats must be sent back.

The Catalan hurried to the upper deck, and whistled. The *Union's* fifty-three men and boys were now drawn up in line within each

bulwark.  They were summarily searched by
the twenty-five who came running from below,
and everything in the shape of a weapon was
taken from them.   Four of the twenty-five
then hurried into one of the boats, took the
other two in tow, and made for their ship.   The
*Huelva* began to smoke, and in a few minutes
started into running between two long wavering
pennants of foam.   In twenty minutes she
vanished from sight twelve miles to the south-
east.

The bow of the *Union*, meantime, had been
turned due north.   She was now in what is
called the Mona Channel, between Porto Rico
and St. Domingo.   The prize-crew was in
charge ; the men of the *Union* were mostly
huddled together toward the fo'castle.   What
was the new destination of the vessel no one,
except the Catalan and two or three of his men,
was aware.

At one bell of the forenoon watch, the
American squadron was sighted in line abreast
at eight cables' interval on the port bow of the
*Union*, heading   east   by   south   along   the
St. Domingo coast near Cape Engano.   The
*Union* passed within a knot of them, showing
the Stars and Stripes.

It was soon after this that a once Sicilian

bandit, happening to pass along the main corridor of the cabin, heard a sound, and stopped to listen. It came from behind a door, and resembled the slow, heavy breathing of someone sleeping. Dick P. Hocking, who had been interrupted in his morning's nap, had let the neglected extinguished cigar slant from his lips, and in the long interval of waiting had lapsed into napping.

The Sicilian listened till there could be no doubt of the accuracy of his hearing ; then he tried the door and found it locked ; then he started to run upward with the news ; and as he started, he dropped with a groan.

A man who had been watching him from behind an angle of the corridor had stepped out briskly and silently, and dropped the weight of a belaying-pin upon the foreigner's temple. He stopped to take a knife with sickle-curved blade from the sheath, and two Colts from the girdle of the fallen man ; then he picked a key from a pocket of his clerical waistcoat, and opened Hocking's door.

' It's about time, I reckon,' he said quickly at Hocking's ear, and flew to the chest. Hocking's lids slowly unrolled themselves, and instantly he was alert and up. At the same time three other men, the captain, mate, and engineer of the *Union*, appeared.   They had come aft under-decks through the space of two planks removed from bulkheads.   And at once the five, Hocking still in his pyjamas, set to work to load the Winchesters, and then hurriedly passed out, bearing between them the twenty-five rifles and a box of ammunition.

The whole length of cabin was deserted. They passed on till they came to the first plank-space in the bulkhead ; and here there was a pause.   Hocking could not get through.

The silent removal of the board had been a matter of considerable difficulty to that militant and resourceful person, Petersen.   The removal of another at this juncture was not to be thought of.

'All right,' said Dick P. Hocking ; 'I'll keep one of the guns, and you go ahead.   I'll join you in my own fashion.'

He deposited the Winchesters which he carried on the other side of the bulkhead, and crept cautiously back to the room which he had left.   Here, with sideward listening head, he waited.

He waited five, ten minutes.   Then there reached him the muffled sound of a great outcry from above.   There were shouts, names called, scurrying feet, Spanish oaths, and then, all suddenly, the prattling, brittle crackle of a musketry-volley, instantly followed by another.

The Americans, twenty-six in number, two of them armed with the dead Sicilian's weapons, had taken their stand just aft of the fo'castle, with a breadth of mast and two considerable heaps of chain in protective opposition; the twenty *Huelva* men were better shielded, and took aim from among the funnels and deck-houses. The non-combatants of the *Union* were below; the vessel lay without forward movement on the water.

Abroad on the deck lay in various curves of death and anguish seven bodies — three Americans, four *Huelva* men. There was a profound silence, save for a hollow sound above the funnels, and the hoarse cry of a flight of boobies afar.

Then suddenly again, from the Spanish side this time, there broke the brittle crackle, the prattling musketry, a whole volley; and as the answer came crackling, the whole forward portion of the ship was rolled in hot reeking smoke and stench, within which men writhed and died.

But now, as the thickness of the powder-fog thinned, it was seen that the Spanish loss was the greater; for at the moment of firing they had exposed themselves unduly, offering their whole bodies as targets, and four had fallen to two on the other side.

There was, however, not the least disposition toward yielding. The Catalan, who was behind the forward funnel, surmising rightly that guns were the Americans' only weapons, hit upon the very best tactical device that could, in the circumstances, be conceived. The thing was to make a rush, and kill at close quarters with knives, daggers and swords.

He called :

' Everyone this way !'

And at once there began a mixed crawling and swiftly-dodging manœuvring of the members of his force toward him. The Rev. Silas M. Petersen, lying at full length behind a coil of chain, and observing a flying lower leg, sent a single shot ; but it splintered the deck beneath the foot.

' When I cry " One !" everyone rush and stab in a body,' said the Catalan.

By this time the American muzzles were resting ready pointed, prepared for the first human limb that showed itself. But the interval between the combatants was not large, and a second's failure to fire on their part might now prove fatal to the whole body, who would be

ONE MAN ONLY TURNED TO KNIFE HIM.

[To face p. 111.

unarmed save for the butt-ends of their not very wieldy guns.

The word 'One' was on the mouth of the Catalan.  He had, in fact, begun to say it, when from behind a shot entered his brain.  It had come from the shoulder of Dick P. Hocking, who had quietly walked forward from the cabin-region toward this point.

One man only turned to knife him, and he was met by the butt-end of Hocking's weapon, which broke open his chest.  Eleven pelted with all speed forward, and as they ran, five dropped.  Hocking stood with projected leg, taking a long, steady second aim, his lips pressed firmly together, the morning air fluttering his pyjamas about his legs.

When he fired, there was already an impassioned stand-up mêlée going on between the contending parties.  It was two or three chances to one that he would hit one of his own men.  But after a long, steady sight, he fired, and a marked Spaniard fell.

It was the sixth gun he had fired in his life. The most craven of his flatterers could never call Dick P. Hocking a brilliant shot.  But he was an efficient man; his name was 'Thorough'; he 'got there,' I guess.

In two minutes the struggle was over.  The

Rev. Silas M. Petersen's face and pastoral
collar ran red, and a long rip went up his palm.
He had fought like three, and the last *Huelvan*
that went down rolled together with Petersen
in a hissing struggle that was ended by a blow
on the Spaniard's nape from the *Union's* mate.
Dick P. Hocking stood contemplating it, and
these things he pondered in his heart.

He was once more master of the *Union*.
He dropped the rifle with a bang.

In half an hour, as the *Union* moved once
more southward to reseek the American fleet,
Petersen approached him with an envelope, all
red.   The parson said :

' One of them had this about him ; I guess
it was to deliver this that they were taking us
northward, and it ought to interest you.'

The envelope under the blood was directed
to Joseph Campos.

Dick P. Hocking sat down at a table, and
he put his spectacles on his nose, and he opened
that envelope.

' This, I reckon, comes under the head of
contraband of war, anyway,' said he.

The chief bulk of the contents consisted of a
piece of parchment, partly printed, and partly
written over in Spanish.   Hocking made out
that it was Immanuel Appadacca's title-deed to

the tract of territory purchased by him contiguous to the disputed boundary-line between British Guiana and Venezuela.

Then there was a letter written in Appadacca's own hand on vellum. It gave to Campos certain detailed instructions as to the winding-up of various business affairs in the United States, as to conveying a sum which he named to the rebel Gomez, and as to Campos' immediate departure for Cadiz, where Appadacca needed him.

But the interest of the letter was in its end. It stated that a certain millionaire, named Immanuel Appadacca, had lately died. He was a Venezuelan, but entertained a profound admiration for England and the English. Moreover, he was a man with whom the mere possession of a whim meant its accomplishment. He had left the disputed Guiana-Venezuelan territory as a free gift to the British Government. The title-deeds were enclosed.

The letter ended with these words :

'I am about to cut the cable between the two British islands of St. Lucia and St. Vincent. You are to spread the report by every means in your power that this act, which constitutes an act of war against Britain, is the work of the Spanish cruisers now in these waters.'

8

# CHAPTER X.

## THE CHAMBERLAIN SPEECH.

DICK P. HOCKING sat long, puzzling over this letter. He understood the meaning of the Spanish words, but he did not understand the letter.

Only, he understood that it meant mischief, earthquake, world-trouble. Also, he understood that all this was proceeding from the intellect of Appadacca ; and by now he had learnt to reverence the intellect of Appadacca.

He called to him the Rev. Silas M. Petersen. He said :

' Look here, parson, just let me translate to you this thing.'

And he translated it, word for word. And when he was finished, there was silence for five minutes, until the reverend gentleman, lifting up a clear brow, said slowly and distinctly :

' It is the sharp nails of—the Woman, I guess.'

'Yes, I can make out that much of it,' said Hocking, scratching his head.

'He says that he wants it to look so that Spain has committed an act of war against England, as I understand. Well, that signifies that he wants England to declare war against Spain, if words have any signification.'

Hocking's abdomen began to dandle in a laugh.

'Ho! that would signify a rather sharp bust-up for Spain, wouldn't it?'

'It would signify a bust-up—yes,' answered Petersen, 'but not a sharp bust-up. Not if Russia, and France, and Germany, and Italy, and Austria, and the rest of Europe took sides with Spain.'

'Damn the rest of Europe!'

'Well, *condemn* the rest of Europe as we may, there Europe stands, a solid fact. And I am only saying that it seems clear to me that that is about what this Appadacca is feeling after. A quarrel between Spain and England at this moment will just signify to the rest that England is siding actively with the States; and just let that word "Alliance" get abroad, and the skies'll blacken, you'll see, and there'll be thunders and lightnings on this earth.'

'Yes; but don't you see, parson, here's the

fellow doing something in just the opposite
sense to his other act : he's actually offering
this piece of land to England.   It's the motive
here that bothers me.'

'Ah, there I don't pretend to perceive the
inwardness of his deal,' said Petersen.   ' It
looks——'

' It *looks* as if he wanted to open old sores
between England and the States.   You know,
parson, that the two nations have forgotten
all about this matter very near — the two
*nations ;* but perhaps you don't know that the
big guns, the people behind the scenes who
run the nations, are a bit sore yet over that
same Venezuelan boxing-match.   It wouldn't
altogether be sugar-plums and cocoanut-water
to Pennsylvania Avenue, Washington, if this
particular piece of land became British territory, I tell you, sonny.'

'On the other hand, he is aiming at throwing
the two nations into each other's arms by his
cable-cutting.   He is either a fool, or a precious
profound sort of rascal——'

'Stop!   I have worked it out, parson,' cried
Hocking, dropping his fist on the table.   ' No,
no, the man isn't a fool ; he's a man worth
fighting with and conquering, is this Appadacca.
Wait—wait.   It's a case of going one better,

is it ? All right, Mr. Señor, with your beastly jokes. Don't you surmise what he is after now, parson ? He wants to make England look so that she seems allied with us, by snarling at Spain ; but he doesn't want it to be a firm and cordial alliance. Between the two friends, just at the critical moment, he throws this bone—not enough, perhaps, to bar the alliance, but enough to make them snarl at each other behind the scenes while they are openly snarling at the common foe. This darned fellow means mischief all round.'

' You've hit it there !' said Petersen.

They nodded at each other.

' Yes ; but this particular bit of land belongs to Dick P. Hocking at the present moment,' said Hocking. ' These title-deeds are contraband of war, if anything is. First I got the ship and he got the land ; now I've got the land and he's got the ship, I guess. We'll see how we go on.'

By noon the deck of the *Union* had been cleared of the dead, and the five wounded were being tended in cabin-berths. At three o'clock the American squadron was again sighted at the southern end of the Mona passage. A boat of the *Union* was sent to the flagship, and information given as to the latitude in which the Spanish ships had been seen, and also as to the sailing of the *Huelva* in the direction of the Spaniards.

It was therefore without much hope of finding the enemy that the Americans continued on their way. Towards sunset of the next day their scouts came in with the announcement that the Spaniards had undoubtedly turned back. Twenty-four hours afterwards Europe learnt that the Spanish cruisers and gunboats were coaling at Martinique, and a few days later at Curaçao.

The Americans, on their part, turned back also. Some of their ships were detailed to watch the Cuban 'Windward' Channel, some hurried to the east end of Cuba to watch the Yucatan Channel, lest the Spaniards should pass that way to fall upon the few unprotected ships maintaining the blockade of Havana ; the rest of the Americans proceeded to San Juan.

Then followed the bombardment. The Americans, entering the bay, poured a red rain upon the wretched forts intended to protect the more wretched town. The San Juan guns were manned by amateurs, untrained enthusiasts, local warriors ; their shots fell wide or short, they did little damage. In England the newspapers printed in bourgeois type 'thrilling' details of this 'terrible' affair. But the important point of the engagement was announced in small nonpareil in sequestered corners. It was this : that at every shot which inflicted 'an insignificant damage upon an American ship, the crew of a small French cruiser in the bay sent up cheer on cheer.

At this time it had been resolved among the ladies of New York to import no more Parisian modes ; and popular feeling against France for her supposed partisanship with Spain had gone so far, that members of the House of Representatives were declaring their determination to oppose any money vote to enable the United States to take part in the Paris Exhibition of 1900.

It was at a time like this that a British Minister of State, and a member of the Cabinet, threw his bomb.

Mr. Joseph Chamberlain, in a public speech, spoke of 'alliance' between the English-speaking races.

It was to be presumed that he spoke with authority, with responsibility. And if so, his words were great in import. It meant the complete upsetting of the balance of power of the world. It meant that Britain would be far stronger than any present combination of force in Europe ; it seemed to invite all the various combinations of force in Europe to become a single combination of force—to put all their weight on the other side of the see-saw—if they were not to be hurled and scattered into the air by this tremendous aggregation of weight.

And at once the Continent took fire. The island threatened to become the dog ; the mainland was dwindling to the tail. Can the tail wag the dog ? Look well to it, ye Powers.

Whether the British Government was aware how events connected with the Spanish-American war were already tending to bring about a European combination against the Saxon race, without the aid of outspoken speeches, is unknown. *With* the aid of outspoken speeches, it was certainly not far off.

Even the Swiss and Belgian press cried out in scare.

On the next morning there was a hurried meeting of the Cabinet Council at Madrid. For one Power to offer alliance to a second at the moment when that second is at war with a third, was not unlike an act of hostility committed by the first against the third.

And to make the cloud darker, just at the beginning of the Cabinet Council, General

Martinez Campos had handed him the following telegram :

'*Huelva* will be at Cadiz during the week, when I hope to confer with you for your guidance. British cable about to be cut will be cut by me.—APPADACCA.'

At the Cabinet meeting it was resolved that at once the Spanish Government should make representations to the various Powers, beginning with Russia, as to the speech of the British Minister, and its obvious effect in upsetting the balance of power in Europe.

And that night, under a dulled moon stooping her head through sombre trails of cloud, a party of men landed on a rocky coast at a southern headland of the island of St. Vincent. The occupant of the stern was wrapped in a flowing mantle, and as the boat's bow touched the gravel where the surf came with spasmodic lap, he was lifted out by a man who stood knee-deep, and deposited on the dry sand. Ten of the twelve who formed the crew then walked along the edge of the curving coast-wall, searching the ground, that cloaked figure last.

In five minutes someone whispered, ' Here it is !'

He pointed to a thick cable made of layers of netted wire, alternating with gutta-percha, which ran down a hillside, then along the sands, then dived to its dark bed within the deep.    A man lifted an adze.

But before it fell, the cloaked figure cast a hurried glance behind.    He had heard a footstep.    The next moment a fat hand was laid lightly on his back.

'Don't you do that,' said a voice.

The other's face paled with passion ; he said not a word.

'Look you,' said Silas M. Petersen ; 'I came all the way over the mountains from Castries to-day on horseback, purposely to stop you in this affair, for I knew beforehand all about it, you can bet.    And I can stop you, for behind those rocks are twenty men, well armed. Well, but I don't mean to stop you.    I have about come round to the view of my kind friend and master, who wants you to work your will in this deal, and take the consequences. Only, hark you, I am a preacher of the Gospel —and stop—are you a priest ?    You are ! Then we are birds of the same quill, I reckon. It's peace and goodwill we are both after, I guess.    That's what we are there for, you'll say : to do the will of the Lord Jesus Christ,

who said, " Blessed are the peacemakers."
Then I counsel you, stop this business, brother.
I won't prevent you, but, if you love your
country, and your own life, stop it.'

Down, once, twice, thrice, fell the adze.

And from the priest's curved and pallid lips
fell one word, the murmured word :

' Vermin !'

And Silas M. Petersen, as he turned away,
he, too, with a certain disdain, said aloud :

' Pride goeth before destruction, my man, and
a haughty spirit before a fall. . . .'

# CHAPTER XI.

## IN DEEP WATERS.

THE *Huelva* coaled at Martinique. She left the south end of St. Lucia, where the cable was cut, without the least suspicion on the part of anyone on board that the *Union*, with Hocking, was at Castries, near the north end.

During the night of the seventh day the *Huelva's* pinnace was throbbing up the Solent with Appadacca in her stern. Late the next afternoon he was closeted with the Prime Minister in an inner apartment at the Foreign Office.

At this time the Anglo-American *rapprochement* was looming large. It was in everyone's mouth.

There was, indeed, the faintest suspicion abroad that the British Prime Minister himself was not so passionately enamoured of alliance as some of his lieutenants, as the mass of the nation, as the mass of Americans. Since the beginning of the movement he had made speeches, but on that subject had remained austerely mute.

It was known that, in general, he had the strongest personal antipathy to the Yankee; but it was supposed that one man, even if he were strongly inclined that way, would be unable to withstand the set of the national currents. Already, in fact, a meeting to settle preliminaries had been arranged to take place in New York between the American Secretary of State, the Assistant-Secretary of State, Sir Julian Pauncefote, the British Ambassador, and Sir Louis Davies, the Canadian Minister of Marine.

The mightiest affairs, however, depend upon the wills and motives of individuals.

'You tell me a strange thing, señor,' said the Prime Minister.

'It is, however, true,' replied Appadacca.

'And the title-deeds, you say, should be in our hands—when?'

'Within nine days at the furthest.'

'It is by no means certain, you know, that our Government will see its way with absolute clearness to accept the gift. I do not conceal from you that we are, most of us, in no mood

at the present moment to give any cause of
jealousy to the people of the United States.
We recognise their war as just and magnanimous——'

'Their very justice is unjust.'

'Ah, you think that——'

'Their very magnanimity is mean.'

'There are those who say so.'

'When a whole nation gives itself up to one
object for a whole century, my lord, and that
object a base one, you will find at the end of
that century, if you observe them narrowly,
that their very pity is tainted, their very truth
is false. They will have generous impulses,
but their very generosity will be a self-decep-
tion. In nothing, nothing, will they be quite
sincere, except in their greed, in their selfish-
ness. In this matter of Cuba, you have a
nation whose sole motto is self-interest, whose
very soul is corrupt with it, whose very name
has become synonymous with callous greed—
this is the nation which you find exclaiming,
with a kind of fictional belief in its own
words: "How admirably magnanimous a one
am I !"'

'I follow you, señor. You, however, miss
my point. I did not say that this war is
magnanimous. But I said that we here in

England—the mass of our nation, magnanimous itself, and judging, of course, only by
the first outside look of things, which is all
they ever get to see—that *they* regard it as
magnanimous.'

'And this view of theirs——'

'Makes our position with regard to this
otherwise most acceptable gift of land a far
from certain one. You are, I presume, the
executor——'

'Informally, yes. The real agent for Señor
Appadacca in the matter is a Señor Josef
Campos, the head of the house of Campos in
New York, of which your lordship may have
heard.'

'And Campos——'

'Will be in England, as I can say positively,
within eight days. He should be now, in fact,
at Cadiz.'

'Then I shall wait the coming of Señor
Campos with some impatience. The matter,
of course, is sufficiently momentous to call for
the summoning of a Cabinet Council ; but
nothing can be done till I have in my possession the title-deeds to lay before my colleagues.
But this gentleman, Appadacca. You knew
him, of course? I seem somehow, or somewhere, to have heard the name.'

'He was the son of a nobleman of Spain. Your lordship probably heard of him in connection with his armed yacht, the *Huelva*.'

'That is so. Now you say it, I remember. And the *Huelva*—will she continue her mysterious voyages ?'

'I cannot say, my lord. If she does, you will be certain to hear of her.'

'But stay. I was very much puzzled a few days ago by reading in the newspapers that a British steamer had reported in New York having sighted some Spanish ships of war near the American coast, when everyone knew that no Spanish ships were in that neighbourhood. Then, if I remember right, two other ships came in and reported the same thing afterwards. It struck me at the time——'

'That the *Huelva* might have had something to do with it ?'

'Just so.'

'It is quite possible, my lord. The captains' imaginations magnified one ship into a fleet; or else the swiftness of the *Huelva's* movements, perhaps, during the night, and her appearance at unexpected points, led them into the belief that it was not one, but several ships which they sighted.'

'And the cutting of the St. Lucia-St. Vincent

cable? Have you any suspicion that the *Huelva* was involved in this matter?'

'On the contrary, my lord.'

The Prime Minister shot an under-glance at Appadacca's face.

'How so?' he said.

'Has your lordship, then, reason to think that the *Huelva* was in those waters?'

'It has been hinted to me.'

'Oh, in that case—but with what motive? Her owner, on the one hand, dowers the British Government with one of the vastest estates in the world. Is it likely that, on the other, he would leave behind him a crew ready for the first act of unprovoked hostility within their reach?'

'Was it, then, señor, an act of the Spanish cruisers?'

'That I admit, though with reluctance, is more probable.'

'Ah—I note the admission.'

'The matter, I hope, is not acutely serious, my lord?'

'It is acutely serious, señor. I give you my word that the affront will not be permitted to pass from sight without due and proper repentance on the part of your country. The unfortunate affair of the *Maine* was, you know,

9

the direct *motif* of the present war ; now comes another similar act, different in form, but identical in a certain spirit of lawlessness, against another nation. One could almost swear that the two acts were performed by the same hand.'

' However, they were not.'

The Prime Minister swept a swift, downward hand on his beard.

' Well, you appear to be more familiar with the details of both matters than I, señor,' he said. 'Are you about to proceed to Spain ?'

' Yes, my lord.'

' Then, you should give them this hint over there : that what is called the British Lion will bear a large amount of horseplay with his tail—until he feels a twinge of pain. And *then* he is very apt to get up, and pile roar on roar in a way that frightens everybody into a disinclination for any more play during a century or so.'

' I will do so, my lord. Personally, I find the roar of the lion exhilarating. I have hunted him in Somaliland with some little success ; off my own camel, assisted by a French, an Italian, and a Russian fellow-huntsman, I have captured—four.'

Once more the Prime Minister swept his

hand down his beard, in a manner characteristic of him.  He said :

' You were quite an international party, then.
The secret of your success seems to me to lie
in the fact that you were united, while the four
lions did not fight together.  The four, joined
into One Big Lion, might have been able to
make short work of that international big-game
expedition, I fancy.'

Appadacca rose.

' The title-deeds shall be in your hands
within the time mentioned, my lord,' he said.

' Well, then—good-day, señor.'

They parted.

# CHAPTER XII.

## THE TITLE-DEEDS.

IMMANUEL APPADACCA at once telegraphed to Cadiz :

'*To* CAMPOS.—Have you arrived? In any case send me word immediately on receiving this.'

He received no answer that night. He was annoyed, but remained in London, in the confident assurance that the next morning he should receive news from Campos, whom he had ordered to Cadiz. The order, written with his own hand, was in the breast-pocket of Dick P. Hoçking.

So were the title-deeds of the frontier estate, without which Appadacca must seem either simpleton or impostor in the eyes of several people.

He had engaged a suite of apartments at the

Hotel Metropole, though his stay was only for a day. He would soon, he knew, be in pressing need of money in specie without the arrival of Campos. He rose early the next morning; there was not a word from Cadiz.

He sent at once a telegram to New York :

' Have you received my instructions and the title-deeds ?'

He waited four, six hours. At last the reply came :

' No ; thought there was something wrong. Await instructions.'

Appadacca wired :

' Charter, if you can, swift craft for Cadiz, and bring all specie at your disposal.'

Then, with knit brow and set lips, he drove to Waterloo. The steam-pinnace of the *Huelva* awaited him at an agreed point of the Hard at Portsmouth.

About two o'clock in the morning he stepped on the deck of the *Huelva*, and at once disappeared below. The bows of the ship turned west, smoke poured from her funnels, and the early break of dawn found her stretch-

ing, like a racehorse in the final heat, at full
speed across the Atlantic.

Appadacca whistled to her captain at about
eight o'clock.

'What is the speed?'

'At the moment thirty-three, your Excellency.'

'How is the wind?'

'On our starboard bow, west by north.'

'I depend upon you, in any case, to arrive
within the time I have prescribed,' said Appadacca.

Now, quite five days previously Dick P.
Hocking had walked up Pennsylvania Avenue;
for, after the cable-cutting, the *Huelva* had
spent three days in forerunning the Spanish
Squadron, and contriving its safe arrival at the
protected port of Santiago de Cuba, a feat of
strategy which, had it been unassisted by the
incalculable movements of such a ship as the
*Huelva*, would have fully justified the exultation
with which the news of the squadron's arrival
was received in Madrid.

Hocking reached the shaded park, and
entered the White House. He sent in a
card marked 'Urgent: ten minutes.' One
of the bamboo screens swung back to admit

him, and he found himself in a scrupulously business-like apartment, in the presence of the President. There was a cordial hand-shaking; a massive chair uttered creaks of distress beneath Hocking's weight.

'I have not much time for palaver,' said Dick P. Hocking. 'Look here, I have had written out for you a description of the present position and so on of our fleet, and the reason why they haven't come aboard those Spaniards yet. The worst enemy America's got at the present moment is not any Spanish squadrons, but one Spanish ship, President; and that, I guess, is what you will be finding before long —that is, if *I* don't come in somewhere. But what I've got to show you chiefly is this little piece of beastly joking. Just you look at that.'

Hocking slapped down the parchment title-deed of the Venezuela estate, and a translation of Appadacca's letter to Campos. Then there was silence for five minutes. The President's eye ran eagerly through the words.

'This means mischief, I calculate,' he muttered.

'It meant,' said Hocking; 'it can't mean any more. That parchment is now in the pockets of the United States, and so is the piece of land it represents.'

'It isn't, Dick P. Hocking,' replied McKinley.
' Look here, don't you fancy that you are going
to get us into any hot places more than we
are in already. That parchment will come
in handy later; it won't go rotten in your
drawers, may be. Right now I beg to decline
it with best thanks.'

' Well, I am not saying that you don't know
your business.'

' No ; you are too cute a man. Look you,
Dick P. Hocking, we have got to be getting
along slow speed and fog-sirens piping these
days in this country ! The motto on the door-
plate of these States has been : " Hands off,
thanks, and let's go our own way in our own
way." And a sound motto it was. Now, all
that is about over, I guess. We have got
mixed somehow in the thick of the row, and
the Almighty only knows what it'll run to.
Here's a document, now : that's a note from
the Italian Government, my son, protesting
against the blockade of Cuba as insufficient.'

' Protesting ?   Why ?'

' *International Law*, Dick P. Hocking.   It's
a spell of international law now that we're in
for, I guess, and the isolation's off, and every
little effete Punch and Judy show of a State in
Europe's beginning to criticise their betters,

because they see that we've been dipping our finger into their dirty little international law pie.   Well, and do you know what ?'

' No.'

' Then I'll tell you : The world's about in for a new era of things right now.   There, on the desk, you see a telegram which gives me to know that an old man is lying at a place called Hawarden, in the West of England, just at his last gasp.   That old man's name is Gladstone, and another way to spell Gladstone is P-e-a-c-e.   When I say that one is at his last gasp, I just mean that the other is too.'

' Yet he retired long ago.'

' Don't you believe that.   There wasn't anywhere for him to retire to, you see, except under the pavement of Westminster Abbey. While he was above it, he was there just the same, I reckon ; and everybody knew he was there, and everybody was afraid of his frown, and of what he would say if they went crooked any.   Retired—no !  He wasn't a snail ; he was a force.'

' And you think——?'

' I think that things look—bad.   I reckon that France and Russia are building too many battleships ; I think that none of those big old nations are strong enough to keep up their swaggering armies another five years. I reckon that England is the best hated nation on the face of the earth; and I reckon the States is in for the row, and has got to take sides whether she wants to or not.'

'I can tell you one thing,' said Hocking: 'it will be a war of races.'

'That's so.'

'Saxon against Latin.'

'Something not far off.'

'We and England——'

'I reckon that's about the combination. If between us we aren't good enough to boss the world——'

'But——'

'Well?'

'Hasn't England everything to gain, and we nothing, by an alliance at this moment?'

'That's so. But there isn't going to be an alliance at this moment. The States wait. But when the day comes, it isn't a matter of small advantage to one or the other that we shall consider, but the general good. Meanwhile, you can see why I tell you to keep your title-deeds in your portfolio. They would be exploding in mine.'

The same night, toward morning, Hocking

arrived at New York. His first care was to
telegraph to the manager of Cramp's shipbuilding works, Philadelphia, desiring a further
immediate interview ; his next was to ascertain
the movements of Josef Campos during the last
few days.

' Has he been realizing largely ?' he asked.

' Apparently not,' said an agent.

' Has he chartered any ship ?'

' I could dare bet no.'

' Then he hasn't heard yet. Appadacca
wants him badly, and will telegraph. The
thing now is to keep him here a prisoner.'

' How could that be managed ?'

' We shall see. Here, parson, just come
and help on this little conference.'

What was certain was that Appadacca, from
the instructions given in his letter to Campos,
needed ready funds for the prosecution of his
schemes. And during the next day several
eyes kept sharp watch upon all the transactions
of Campos.

Then came Appadacca's telegraphic sum-
mons ; and the fact of its arrival was known
to Dick P. Hocking with a certainty as absolute
as though he had read it. The deals of Campos
revealed all.

Campos sought next to obtain a ship ; and

there, with a shock of dismay, he found himself foiled. None of the Transatlantic boats sailed for two days, and his orders were instant and urgent. He was instructed, moreover, to leave by a privately-chartered boat, but no boat could he find to charter.

After a day's scurry among the shipping agencies of New York and Brooklyn, a confidential clerk came to acquaint him with failure.

' There is some mystery in it, you may be certain,' said the clerk.

' A plot of Hocking's ?'

' That, and nothing less.'

' We shall obtain a ship at Newport ?'

' If all the disposable ships at Newport have not been got at in the same manner.'

' Then at Boston or Baltimore ?'

' Would it not be better to telegraph your dilemma to his Excellency ? Boston, I firmly believe, and Baltimore, too, will offer us nothing.'

And with this suggestion Campos at once fell in. He telegraphed to Appadacca at London. He got no reply.

Appadacca was on his way in the *Huelva*. His powers of divination had led him to suspect that, supposing his letter and the title-deeds had reached the hands of Hocking, Hocking would adopt the very ruse which he did in fact adopt with respect to Campos. Hence, in the act of telegraphing for Campos, he felt fairly certain that Campos would not come. He was ignorant that the ship captured by the *Huelva* in the Mona Straits was the *Union*, or that Hocking was on board of her; but he had a suspicion amounting to certainty that documents so important to himself, once miscarried, could hardly fail to reach the hands of Dick P. Hocking.

During two days the brows of Josef Campos were a continual wrinkle of vexation. The whole man grilled with suppressed rage.

At last he lost restraint. He went to Hocking's office; Hocking was not there. He went to Fifth Avenue; Hocking was not there.

'Where is your master?' he asked of a footman.

'He is at Bellevue for some days,' said the man.

Bellevue was one of Hocking's country seats, half-way between New Haven and Providence —a very lonely pile, overlooking a stretch of sea, and standing in its own wide parks.

'I am going at once to Mr. Hocking's seat

of Bellevue,' said Campos to his head-clerk.
'In two hours I shall return. Meantime, if
there be sudden news from his Excellency, you
will not fail to follow me.'

He took train, and in an hour was at
Bellevue. Dick P. Hocking had just ended
a conference of three, consisting of himself,
an agent from Cramp of Philadelphia, and an
agent from the Union Works of San Francisco.
By this time he was something of an authority
on the technicalities of torpedo-boat and torpedo-
destroyer building.

'Show Mr. Campos right in,' he said to the
man who made the announcement.

And while Campos was coming, he blew
through a whistle communicating with the
Rev. Petersen's apartments ; and even as
Campos appeared, he was whispering into
Petersen's ear :

'I don't know that it will be necessary, but
it may—I'll see.   If it is, I'll whistle twice, and
you'll know what to do.   Sit down, señor—sit
down,' he added.

The brow of Campos was flushed with
anger.

'Why this unlawful persecution, Mr. Hocking ?' he said.

'The weather is beginning to warm up at

last, señor. Which unlawful persecution do you refer to ?'

'There is no necessity to beat about the bush, Mr. Hocking. What you have done I know well. I come to inquire into your motive, that is all. *Why* do you seek to prevent me from leaving this country ?'

'Well, now, that's talking straight out, and I like a man who talks straight out. I'll tell you : I have happened to tumble on the fact that your master, Appadacca, or whatever he is to you, is making for some queer mischief, in which he can't very well get along just now without you. So I keep you.'

'I see. Mischief which concerns you personally ?'

'No, no ; not particularly me. But when a man gets to my age and weight, he begins to think of other things besides his own five-cent. affairs. Appadacca isn't going to get along anyhow with Dick P. Hocking pulling the other way.'

'But you speak precisely like a simpleton !' cried Campos in surprise. 'You might as well try to check the momentum of Niagara, as seek to balk the purposes of the man against whom you are absurdly ranging yourself. He is a gentleman—a prince! I tell you, for I know.'

Dick P. Hocking's abdomen dandled upward in a laugh.

'Don't be frightening me now, señor,' he said; 'if I faint in your arms, you'll be sinking under the strain, I reckon.'

'But it is ridiculous!' cried Campos in a high pitch of voice. 'You are merely wasting good money in keeping me here. You merely retain me for a day or two—you might guess that. The *Huelva* is now on her way to America to fetch me.'

'She'll have hell's bells knocked out of her bottom if she comes anywhere across New York Harbour, señor.'

'*If*, perhaps.'

'But you are sure she's coming, eh?'

'Practically—a telegram of mine to his Excellency having remained unanswered.'

'Oh, very good. But when she comes, I'm darned if she finds *you !*'

'I do not follow you.'

'I am going to ask you to be my guest for the next three days or so. I promise you that you will find Bellevue a more hospitable place of residence than *I* found the *Huelva.*'

'You mean that you will keep me here by force?'

'That's what it comes to, I reckon; as your

head man kept me.   All's fair in war, for that matter.'

Hocking rose and blew twice through the telephone whistle.

' However, you will bitterly regret this, you ruffian !' cried Campos.

' I don't say it's impossible, señor.   But look you, I will act above-board to you ; you shall know at least that I have an honest motive in this affair.   Just cast a glance at that.'

As he spoke he had opened a cabinet, taken out the title-deeds of the Venezuela estate, and Appadacca's letter to Campos, which was attached to the deed by an elastic band.   He handed the letter to Campos.

' Now tell me if you call that a right piece of business,' said Hocking.

Campos read the letter.

' But how—how, in the name of Heaven, did you obtain this ?'

' Well, you see, your master was sending it to you in my own ship, which he had seized with his beastly *Huelva*.   I simply got back my ship by killing the crew he sent aboard. Both ships are mine, if it comes to that.   And the land's mine, too, you may bet.   But he can keep his beastly *Huelva* till I'm ready to deal with her.'

'Thank you. You have made much clear to me. And I am your prisoner, you say—for how long?'

'Call it prisoner, if you see fit. Guest is what it is. And for as long as you choose. Four or five days, any way. Till then I guess you don't find many open exits from this house. If you'll follow me, I'll point out your lodging for the time; and if you've a conscience, as you have, no doubt, I guess you won't be saying that I'm exceeding what a man should do in the case.'

'But, in Heaven's name, what right——'

'Oh, right enough, right enough. War 'll come; it's coming faster than any of you think, and plenty of it, and loud. Only Appadacca shan't make it come any quicker than it wants to, if what Dick P. Hocking says goes any.'

He rose, nodded his head, made a motion, and stepped forward. Campos glanced rapidly round the room, and, smiling, followed.

Campos was conducted to a third floor. He was ushered into a complete suite of five rooms luxuriously furnished. One of them looked by three windows over a sloping lawn at the back of the house, the lawn plunging steeply twenty yards away into a large-treed park.

At about midnight, when the house was absolutely quiet, Campos went from room to room, searching in the drawers of the looking-glasses and the ornaments of the dressing-table for pins. He found a few.

From the top of a sofa he took a bright-yellow Japanese cloth. In his pocket was a dark-red handkerchief, which in shadow had quite the look of black. With the pins he had found he pinned the handkerchief in the central space of the saffron cloth. He had now a flag with the *Huelva* colours.

The night was very still. He opened a window, and there was hardly a breath. To the inner and upper framing of the window he attached the cloth by means of his last three pins, leaving it to hang; and immediately behind it he moved a table, on which he placed a lamp. The jalousies he left open. As seen from the garden, the light made quite luminous the colour-contrast between the dark red and the light yellow.

Campos sat near the window. The time passed.

At half-past twelve he began to nod. At one he rose, pacing restlessly. At half-past one he was fast asleep. Near two he heard something resembling a whistle. He looked out cautiously.    There was a man below, looking up.

The night was dark, but not too dark for Campos to recognise the general form of this person.    It was not an enemy; it was a friend—his clerk, Francisco.    Campos lifted the lamp, and showed his own face in clear light.

Francisco talked.    Campos could not hear.

' A little louder,' he said in a strong whisper.

Francisco could not hear.

' I do not hear you,' he said in a strong whisper.    ' The *Huelva* has arrived.'

' It is impossible to hear,' said Campos.

' What do you say ?' whispered Francisco.

Campos took down the cloth, unpinned the handkerchief, took from his pocket a penknife, and began cutting both cloth and handkerchief into very thin strips.    He held up the lamp to show Francisco what he was doing.    When he had obtained about forty strips he tied them together, and he lowered the string with the words scribbled on a note-book leaf :

' I am a prisoner.'

After a few minutes the string was tugged. He drew it up.    It was tied round two leaves of telegrams, and a note from Francisco.

The telegrams were from Appadacca.

Francisco said :

' I received telegram summoning you to join *Huelva* at Halifax (see telegram). Wired that you were probably a prisoner, and where, and reasons why you were there. Received telegram ordering me to convey to you instructions at all costs to secure title-deeds to land. This urgently wanted. You to be rescued to-morrow night (see telegram). Let me know if you will be able to secure title-deeds.'

And Campos, having carefully read the note and the telegrams, pondered for a minute. Then he wrote on a leaf :

' To your question—yes.'

And this he lowered.

# CHAPTER XIII.

## THE NIGHT.

THE man beneath the window moved down the slope of the lawn into the forest. Josef Campos drew up the string, hid it, put out his light, and went to bed.

In Bellevue he fared quite sumptuously the next day. No repayment of *Huelva* starvation here, but, on the contrary, a rather crude plenty —the wines good, but not *recherché;* the fish costly in species, but indifferent in specimen ; everything large and liberal and decent, nothing exquisite and high-toned.

'Here is a being,' thought Campos, 'who can speculate better than he can dine, and fight better than he can eat.'

Dick P. Hocking would have admitted it with pride, but Campos thought it with scorn.

Perhaps the only implements of perfectly civilized man will be the table-knife, the fork, the curling-tongs, and harmless varieties of the plough, such as the needle, and the needle's wife and helpmeet, the thimble. Meanwhile, blessed is the man who has handy the Maxim, the Martini, the Nordenfeldt, and the Tape-machine.

But though Campos missed his chef, and the good things nibbled in the *Huelva*, he dined largely ; and his sense of gratitude did not sufficiently realize the fact that he was a prisoner, or it might have been greater. The suite of apartments in which he found himself formed a sort of flat, of which the rather massive hall-door was double-locked.

He spent the entire day in devising his escape.

It was necessary for him, by midnight, to have the title-deeds to the Venezuela estate in his hands, and to place in the window his lamp as the signal that he had them.

Reviewing the whole matter now, he saw that his promise to obtain them had been rash ; that his attempt to obtain them must necessarily be as ticklish as possible—if he was able to make it at all.

He waited. By half-past ten the house was quiet. He stood at the locked door, listening. No sound. Dick P. Hocking was an early elephant—to that fact he attributed his 'success.'

At a few minutes after eleven Campos set to work.  He took off his boots, and lifted a small table into the passage, or narrow hall, ended by the door.  He put the table against the door, and on it he stood.

His plans were formed with all the adroitness characteristic of the Southern- Latin races of Europe—an adroitness in which, in truth, as the Rev. Petersen said, there is something feminine, something of woman's wit.

As one of the *plats sucrés* of his dinner, he had had a thick-crusted, rather doughy apple-pie, and a large piece of that crust he had secreted.  Of this, when he found himself alone for the night, he had managed, with the help of water, to make a mass which formed an excellent adhesive paste.

He had also been provided that morning with a copy of the rabidly anti-Spanish *Journal*, and a leaf of the *Journal* he now tore into an oblong about two-thirds the size of the pane of orange-coloured glass which stood above the upper horizontal joist of the door.  This leaf he glued with his paste to the inner surface of the glass.  He got down from the table, washed his hands, and waited a quarter of an hour.

He was in a state of great excitement.  His

hands trembled ; but his purposes were quite
definite and clear, and he proceeded to their
execution without hesitation.

He had on one of his fingers a many-faceted
and very large diamond of the purest water.
He remounted the table, and with an edge of
the diamond cut the glass round the edge of
the pasted paper, taking care to cut the bottom
of the oblong flush with the timber above the
door.

With such scrupulous care did he proceed
that it was twenty minutes before he gave a
sharp inward pull at the paper, of which he
had left an unpasted border for the fingers.
The oblong of glass cracked, and came slanting inwards upon his two arms. He coaxed it,
it disengaged itself wholly ; he deposited it on
the table ; in a minute he was a free man on
the other side.

He began to run with thievish care through
the darkness ; he heard a clock in a passage
strike with dreadful loudness a quarter to
twelve ; he was very late.

He knew exactly his way to the cabinet
which was his aim ; he had noted it minutely
on his passage to his quarters.

He slid swiftly down some broad-carpeted
stairs, along two passages, then, with the

slowest caution, he turned a handle and entered a bedroom. Now there was sound —the loud slumber of Dick P. Hocking. At one end of the chamber burned a nimbused *veilleuse* in feeble loneliness. Campos saw Hocking lift his stiff beard, and scratch the neck beneath in sleep.

He passed through by another door, then across a dining-room, stumbling over a chair, and down a corridor, and half-way along this he stopped and tried a handle.

He had luck ; the door opened.

As he entered, a feeling of security and success possessed him. He knew even the tool by which he would be able to do his work. It was a short, sharp-pointed poker of brass, which lay with a larger one in the fireplace. But even as he went to seek for it he started : the melancholy gong of a clock in the room clanged and shivered. It was twelve, and Appadacca was as punctual as the moon and the tides.

He set flurriedly to work : struck a match, found the poker, struck another, found the lock in the cabinet, and in a moment the point was working and rummaging in the hole.

He evidently knew his way ; his work was deft, swift, and almost noiseless. With a little pop and outburst the small square door flew back. Campos inserted his hand and felt the papers, and as he did so started. Suddenly the room was full of light.

He spun like a wind-smitten weather-cock, the papers gripped like death in his hand ; and there at the door he saw in nightshirt and fat, short trousers, and slippers too big for him, the Rev. Silas M. Petersen, holding a lamp, gazing at him.

They faced each other, Campos very white, Petersen looking far sideways on the ground in a severe, surprised, judicial way, quite cool.

' This, I guess, is what you'd name knocking pieces out of the rights of hospitality, señor,' he said.

And as he said it, Campos was at him. Seizing the parson by the arm, the Spaniard dragged him into the room with a sudden tug which brought Petersen stumbling, and sent the lamp flying from his grasp.

And in the darkness Campos rushed to the key, turned it, and put it into his pocket ; then to another door nearly opposite rushed, turned the key, and put it into his pocket.

At the same moment Petersen was whistling through the telephone-tube ; and almost as soon as Campos had secured the second key,

a responsive whistle whiffed in the room ; and
Petersen cried :

' Here right now, sir !   The Spaniard is here
purloining *the deeds !*'

He had hardly screamed the words, when he
flung himself upon Campos.

There was a hint of obscure light in the
room through a half-open window, though the
night without was dark, and rain was falling in
sullen, heavy drops.

Campos no longer had the papers in his
hand.   He had with a swift movement deposited them beneath a chair ; but the aim of
Petersen was one of the large door-keys quite
palpable in the trouser-pocket of Campos.

And now ensued a panting struggle among
tumbling chairs and the cracking lamp, Petersen
heaving and slanting the slim body of Campos
in the strain to effect a throw, and Campos,
grinning with effort, forcing Petersen backward
by the hair on both sides of the temple.   It
was only when it was clear that the parson was
much the tougher of the two, and the floor
was dancing from side to side under Campos'
struggling toes, that, at the moment before his
fall, the Spaniard made a sudden effort and
lurch toward the window, and away went both
keys flying through the air.

Outside a gruff, rough voice was heard.

' Hi, there! What's the meaning of this?
—you and your beastly jokes! Open the door,
there!'

' The man has thrown away the keys. He
has the title-deeds——' began Petersen, and
stopped suddenly in wild surprise.

A singular sound was heard from some
short distance. It was a sound of cannon—the
steady, sharp jabbering of a quick-firing gun.

In the room was silence, without it no sound,
save that panting, intense bang-bang, bang-
bang. The three men stood listening, Hocking,
with sideward head and frowning brow, his
heavy eyelids making small his eyes.

Then all at once there was a cracking row,
the ripping of woodwork, and the ponderous
downfall of something.

' His friends, I reckon,' cried Petersen,
' breaking in the front-door! You should call
up the servants and—quick—the villagers!'

The ' villagers' consisted of some three
hundred operatives, engaged on the steel-works
of Hocking and Dorst at Chickville, a mile
and a half away.

By the time Hocking could turn to run, there
was audible a scattered tread of feet in the
house below.

As he panted along a passage, he met about ten servants, some of them women, cowering and inquisitive.

'Every Jack of you,' cried Hocking, 'get pokers—anything you can grip—ah, some of you have already—and knock the bottom out of that door. And you, Jane, get right to the village, and tell the men to come with any weapon they can grip.'

He himself snatched an iron bill from the hand of a girl; some ran to seek clubs of wood in the kitchens; the rest followed him to one of the locked doors, and at once a battering hail of strokes began to bump upon it.

Above the noise was heard the voice of Josef Campos crying shrilly in Spanish:

'Hi! hi! I am here!'

The sound of the straggling, wandering footsteps had died in this tumult, though, in reality, they had come nearer; but for a time the invaders were unable to locate the spot. The loud bombardment of Hocking and his servants continued; the door began to start and spring inward at the continued stress of blows. Presently outside the other door a quiet voice said in Spanish: 'It is here.'

And instantly at this other door began a second furious hammering, and the two, raging

THE REV. PETERSEN, WITH A DIVING RUSH, PASSED THROUGH IT.

[*To face p.* 159.

together upon the two doors, filled all the house with uproar.

It became a question of moments which of the two sets of besiegers would succeed in forcing entry. They were separated from sight of each other by a wall.

It soon became certain, however, that the later set of besiegers were both more numerous and were battering with heavier implements—with the butt-ends of their rifles, namely; and in perhaps three minutes at this door there was a crackle and crash, and two shoulders which had been urging together near the lock tumbled in with the sudden flight of the woodwork.

Now light from two ship's hand-lanterns streamed in. But as the door flew inward, the Rev. Petersen, with a diving rush, passed through it, and, before they could seize him, drove beyond the small crowd without.

Someone said above the noise :

' Señor Campos.'

And Campos said : ' Your Excellency.'

' You have the deeds ?'

' Yes.'

' Then to the shore instantly with them.'

It was then that the second door crackled and burst in. Dick P. Hocking, huge in his pyjamas, appeared.

A man with a mask over his brow and nose said in a hurried whisper to Campos :

'Quick! Take the men with you.'

Campos was already at the door, the deeds in his hand. The man in the mask stood in the way of Hocking. Campos slipped through.

As the man turned to follow the last of his own side, Dick P. Hocking sidled with a swift movement, and barred his way.

'Guess you don't,' he said.

At this time there was very little light in the room—only that of a very small bedroom lamp, held by one of the servants. The whole of the individuals composing the other party had gone, taking the ship's lanterns. The man in the mask was left alone with Hocking and the servants. He found his passage barred.

The *Huelva* party—for the *Huelva* lay in the offing—consisted of twelve. They had brought with them a small quick-firing gun, mour';ed on a pedestal on wheels, with which they had demolished the hall-door, on missing the preconcerted signal which Campos was to place in the window. As they came down again, Campos in their midst now, their first thought was of the gun. It had been left on the lawn when it had been used. But now it had vanished.

They scattered to seek it among hedges and tree-clumps, and in this fruitless task spent some minutes. And even while they were so engaged, they heard a tramp of running feet and a shout.

The Rev. Petersen, on making his escape, had rushed down to bring Chickville out upon the invaders. He had only stopped to wheel the gun into a hidden grotto at the edge of the park ; then, as fast as his short legs could carry him, set off for Chickville.

He met them half-way, coming. They had been roused by a servant from Bellevue. Petersen put himself at their head. They were forty workmen, who had hurriedly snatched some sort of weapon, and rushed out half-dressed.

As they entered the open space of lawn, they sent up a shout, and were joined by the servants of the house, who issued from a side-door. And the whole body scattered in twos and threes, making for the individuals oı the Spanish party, who, too, were scattered in search of the gun.

The Spaniards, outnumbered and hopelessly demobilized, took at once to their heels, firing as they went. All round the undulating spread of lawn rose thickly-wooded land, and into this, at various points on one side of the house and the other, the thirteen vanished, three of the Chickville workmen having first fallen, dead or wounded.

The only course now open to the Spaniards, who had no preconcerted signal for meeting, and were lost to each other, was to make their way, each man for himself, through the trees toward the seashore.   And Petersen, imagining that precisely this was what they would do, hurried with his following down in that direction, patches of smoke breaking out at odd spots along the edge of the trees.

They reached the shore with the loss of only one man more, however.   Then looked for the boat ; and could just discern it a cable-length from the shore, well beyond their reach. Yonder, over the water, a red port-light.

As for the Spaniards in the wood, they found themselves cut off from the boat, and without the power of mobilizing themselves in the absence of either leader or signal.   This thought occurred to some, ' Where on earth *is* our leader ?'

Appadacca was face to face with Hocking. They were alone.   Hocking was opposing the egress of Appadacca.

' Guess you stop here, you rascal,' Hocking said.

'I warn you, however, that it is dangerous
to oppose my passage,' said Appadacca.

'To the devil with your warnings! And be
marvelling at my mother's gentleness in not
cleaving your head with this chopper right
now.'

'You refuse me passage?'

'Refuse! Ay; you and the race of you,
with your beastly jokes.'

He said it with ineffable contempt.

Appadacca did not reply, or his reply was a
red flash of something in Hocking's eye. He
had struck a fusee, which filled the apartment
with a rosy glare.

It was now that Dick P. Hocking for the
first time saw him clearly. And, seeing him,
he started. Here was the mask, and the very
cloaked-figure of the man who had one night
mysteriously fed him in his hunger.

He was so possessed and impressed by the
recognition that for the moment surprise kept
him from interfering with the proceedings of
the unknown man ; and during that moment
Appadacca had lighted a small rocket, had
rushed to the window, and was holding the
spouting and soaring flame out in the open
night.

It was seen by all the Spaniards on both

sides of the house, most of them being now far down in the neighbourhood of the shore; it was seen also on board the *Huelva*, and from her two boats at once put off.

And here was the signal which the Spaniards needed for their renewed mobilization. Immediately each man, knowing that each of the others would do that very thing, rushed from his lurking-place, the whole making half toward the house, and half toward the centre of the lawn at its back; and near here they met, and went running toward the spot of the rocket, where some belated sparks still slowly fell. Behind them came the hue and cry of the villagers and servants from the shore.

Campos had joined in this run; he borrowed a clasp-knife from one of the sailors. In his breast-pocket were the title-deeds.

At the moment when the Spaniards entered the house, the struggle between Appadacca and Dick P. Hocking was nearly over. It was fought with a cat-o'-mountain fury in that dark room, the Spaniard showing his teeth, the American heaving in persistent, unconquerable effort. There came a moment when Appadacca, freeing his right hand, buried a small curved cangiar in the American's shoulder, and at the same instant was impelled backward by a heavy

TWO MUZZLES POINTING AT HOCKING'S HEAD.

[*To face p.* 165.

blow in the chest. As his back staggered against the wall, the whole weight of the American pressed over him ; his right hand was gripped in Hocking's left, and Hocking's iron bill was held aloft, ready to descend.

Appadacca seemed at his mercy. Yet the bill paused before it descended, and when it descended, descended harmlessly.

' Now we are about quits,' panted Hocking.

And while the clock might tick twice, there were rapidly-approaching footsteps, light in the room, two muzzles pointing at Hocking's head.

Appadacca, the mask still covering his face, held up a forefinger. The muzzles dropped. Hocking hurriedly scratched his chin, hesitating, pricked, puzzled.

And now came near the sounds of the running villagers, and the shrill voice of Silas M. Petersen was heard.

Appadacca saw Campos, and said angrily :

' What are you doing here ?'

Before he could receive a reply, an indescribable mêlée, fought with every manner of weapon, commenced. In the packed passage outside the room there were crackling guns and shouts, and cracking heads, and the smiting of clubs on the partition, and struggling feet, the men of the *Huelva* fighting like tigers, the men of the village like veterans.

It could not, however, have lasted more than two minutes, when from behind the villagers there came a fresh crackling of musketry, with dying cries, and loud confusion rolled in smoke, and smell of burning wood.  Then there was a shout from Josef Campos, crying, ' Back ! back !' and the gruff growl of Hocking, ' Stop fighting !'   And in a minute each man was running for himself, and the corridor shot out tongues of flame.

The Spaniards hurried down the stairs, and out to the front of the house, which was the end furthest from the shore.

There they formed, and at a quick march set out for the beach.   The three boats were waiting now near the surf.

Behind a tree near by crouched Petersen, who had escaped from the house by the back. In the stern of one of the boats sat a lank, cloaked figure.

The Spaniards began to jump into the boats. Appadacca had already been lifted into one of them and been rowed away ; five men only were left on the shore ; one of them was Josef Campos.

He happened to be standing by himself a

moment before being lifted into the third of the boats, when from behind a tree near a swift figure darted out upon him with such intense impetuosity that, before Campos knew of its advance, he was on the ground. With such skilled precision had Petersen chosen his opportunity, that his feat of consummate audacity was successful before he was even perceived by anyone. He had the deeds in one hand, and in the fingers of the other the windpipe of Campos, stifling his cry.

But as he leapt up, Campos shouted; and the lank figure in the boat had a night-glass at his eyes.

'There, there!' he cried; 'pick me down that man quickly, one of you!'

Petersen, as he ran, dropped. The smoke cleared, and the priest, with the glass at his eyes, said:

'Let him be brought on board the *Huelva*, if he still lives.'

The three boats passing over the sea, weltered through a red of blood, thrown abroad by the flames of Bellevue.

# CHAPTER XIV.

## ORGANIZING A VICTORY.

APPADACCA had promised the British Prime
Minister that the title-deeds should be in his
hand on the ninth day. In spite of the fact
that it had been necessary for the *Huelva* to
coal outside Halifax from a collier which she
molested, and for him to regain the deeds by
grim fight, he was able to present himself at
the Foreign Office during the afternoon of the
promised day.

At this time he was alone in England, the
*Huelva* being already far on her way to San
Sebastian. In a room of her cabin sat the
Rev. Silas M. Petersen, and opposite him on
a couch reclined Father Pedro. Petersen's
wounded leg lay on another chair, his trousers
pulled above the bulky roll of white ban-
daging.

'The books I have given you,' said the

priest, ' I shall expect you to read with all the intelligence at your command.'

Petersen nodded.

' I'll read them,' he said.    ' Guess the look of them is a trifle heathenish, all the same.'

' I have taken this interest in the salvation of your soul,' said the priest, ' because you once quoted a passage of Scripture to me, with little comprehension of its meaning, I fear, and because, in fact, I choose to do so.'

' Well, I am not for saying that your meaning, though mistaken, is not a praiseworthy one,' said Petersen.

' If difficulties should arise in your mind as you read,' went on the priest, ' you will apply to me.    By faith, and prayer, and humility, every obstacle will be found to vanish.'

' That's so,' said Petersen.    ' Myself, I guess I'll count the time on board this yacht a well-spent season if I am made the blessed means of plucking you from the burning, old gentleman, and guiding you into the way of a real and saving faith in the Lord Jesus Christ.'

The priest looked at the man under his eyes, stroking down his silver crucifix with his fore-finger.

' That, however,' he said, ' is hardly the spirit in which I wish, and expect, you to peruse the works which I have selected for your correction and conversion. The grace of humility—constant prayers for that I recommend to you as your first and chief orison.'

'Right you are there. Don't you go thinking that I am saying that I need it any less than you, old gentleman. I guess the old Adam is in about all of us—not a bit more in you than in me. If I could only put you in the same way of squelching him which I have found to the joy of me heart——'

The priest rose. He could not hide the nausea on his curling lip.

'Don't you be going right now,' said Petersen. 'There is that verse in the third chapter of St. John which I want to lay before you——'

The priest stalked three paces, stopped, and turned. His face was severe, his lips pressed.

'You must pray for humility,' he said.

'I will,' said Petersen; 'I will pray for humility to be given to you.'

'And I, on my part, will pray for it for *you*, sir. And *my* prayer will be answered, for you shall be humbled.'

'Those only who exalt themselves shall be humbled, old gentleman. That's the promise, and self-exaltation isn't in my line of business, any way. You think I exalt myself, when I'm only working for your immortal soul's good ; and there's where you mistake me.   However, we'll be understanding each other better later on, I reckon.'

'Meantime, it is my will that you read——'

'I will ; and on that you may rely.   The verse is in the third chapter, beginning, "Except a man be born——"'

Father Pedro was gone.   Petersen sat and commenced to read.

The next morning the *Huelva* reached San Sebastian.   Father Pedro made haste toward Madrid, where he had three long private interviews with Señor Sagasta, Martinez Campos, and the Queen, before he again set off northward for Paris.

On the third noon he was closeted at one of the Government offices in the Place de la Concorde with M. Hanotaux.   He presented an informal letter from the Queen Regent.

'What you have in mind, señor,' said the Foreign Minister, 'is on the programme of destiny.   I speak frankly.   It is too momentous to be brought about by any one man or nation, to be hindered by any one man or nation. Events have prepared it—it will be.'

'But when, monsieur ?'

'The apple falls when it is ripe, señor.'

'Or it may be plucked.'

'That is an alternative, certainly.'

'By the time the apple is ripe, monsieur, Spain may be no longer there.'

'Yourself have said that it may be plucked, señor.'

'How?'

'Nothing can be done for Spain till she does something for herself.'

'What, monsieur?'

'She must organize a victory.'

'One?'

'One will be sufficient.'

'And with what motive?'

'This : a recovery of her collapsed prestige. Europe will not intervene on behalf of nothing, will not be urged to union and movement on behalf of nothing. Spain must show herself something — a virile, living, more or less successful nation—before she can command our overt sympathy or aid. Let her do this, and that will be one step—perhaps the only one necessary — towards the plucking of the apple.'

'I follow you. But this victory, monsieur —is it possible, practicable?'

'Oh, distinctly. It needs only organization.'

'If you will hint to me in what direction——'

'When will you see Señor Appadacca, Father Pedro?'

'Soon.  Within three days, if necessary.'

'He is——'

'In England.'

'You should telegraph to him, and tell him you heard me say the word " Santiago." '

'Then you think——?'

Hanotaux bowed.

'I think the situation at least promising, Father.'

'But the blockading ships greatly outnumber the blockaded.'

'Not greatly, I think.  Add to the side of the blockaded such a tool as the *Huelva*, and such a brain as her master's, and, if I am a judge, Spain will vindicate her right to existence in the eyes of Continental Europe.'

'Then I shall at once fulfil your recommendation, monsieur,' said the priest, rising.

'Well, then, Father Pedro, I counsel haste, while the situation is *in statu quo*—and this time there should be no failure.'

Father Pedro within the hour wired Appadacca from Paris a long telegram in cipher. It arrived at a moment when Appadacca received also the news that a telegram had been sent from New York to the London Foreign

Office, warning it of the fact that the gift presented to it by the supposed dead man was, in reality, a bait offered by a living person called Appadacca, for motives inimical to both the British and American nations. The information was conveyed to Appadacca by an under-secretary in a cold note of a few lines. He recognised the hand of Dick P. Hocking. And when the telegram from Don Pedro was placed before him, he had already said to himself that very word—'Santiago.'

At this time Commodore Schley had been already five days blockading, in the land-locked harbour of Santiago, five first-class Spanish cruisers and two destroyers with the battleships *Texas*, *Massachusetts*, and *Iowa*, the cruisers *New Orleans*, *Marblehead*, and *Brooklyn*, and the torpedo-boat *Porter*. Santiago had, in fact, been the point to which the long dodging and manœuvring of the Spanish, aided as it had been by the great yacht, had been directed. The entrance was only a little over a couple of hundred feet wide, was long and winding, thick with mines, and dominated by forts with modern guns.

Appadacca replied to Don Pedro's message in the words :

'Shall await *Huelva's* pinnace on the Hard

at Portsmouth on Thursday night. See Sagasta,
and make necessary arrangements.'

It was necessary for the priest to return to
Madrid.   There he had left Silas M. Petersen
on Petersen's parole to make no attempt at
escape.

On the second day they travelled together to
Valladolid, by which time Petersen had won
from the priest, by means of a particular display
of interest in the doctrines of the Church, the
fact that Santiago was the point of their next
aim.

And at Valladolid, Petersen, as he sauntered
on a tour of inspection round the town, sent
this telegram in an easy figure-cipher :

'*To* DICK P. HOCKING, New York.—Have
reason to think that situation is about to be
forced at Santiago.   Take steps.'

# CHAPTER XV.

## SANTIAGO.

By the time the *Huelva* reached the neighbourhood of Santiago de Cuba, Admiral Sampson's squadron had unexpectedly joined Commodore Schley's—unexpectedly, both to Schley and to everyone else.

Sampson had been guarding the Yucatan Passage, when he received sudden sealed orders by a despatch-boat from the Navy Department. The truth was, that the message from Valladolid, communicated by Dick P. Hocking, had caused a stir at the Navy Department : ' The situation about to be forced.' At the game of ' organizing a victory ' both sides could play.

As for Dick P. Hocking, he had conceived the bold idea of himself some day fighting a naval battle ; meantime, he had a strong will to see one. The *Union* got under way.

So it came about that by the time the *Huelva* reached the neighbourhood of Santiago, there were some twenty ships of war of various sizes blockading the narrow harbour-entrance, and prepared for any counter-move.

In two days it was given out in New York that the destruction or capture of the Spanish squadron was certain. That they could escape from the harbour—that they could even hold communication with the open sea—seemed impossible.

The harbour mouth, as we have said, is not more than two hundred and fifty feet wide at its narrowest ; along the cañon it was defended by forts like Morro Castle, and Forts Estrella and Socopa, some fitted with quite modern guns, some of the batteries masked. There were lines of torpedoes. The entire winding passage was said to be mined. Within, the land opens into a wide spread of still water, capable of holding craft of the draught of a 14,000-ton battleship. Further inward, the town spreads far upward, rising in terrace on terrace of lovely landscape to the blue distance, where it is backed by the towering ridges of the Sierra Maestra chain.

During the day the American ships coasted slowly within two thousand yards of the shore.

At night the smaller craft were left on guard, and the big cruisers and battleships retired to the deeper sea.

For this there was a pressing reason : with the Spanish fleet were two destroyers, extremely fast, and in the night terrible to the imagination.

Yet seven days passed, and nothing happened. The destroyers lay at anchor. Over Santiago brooded a horrible silence, a baleful uneventfulness.

In the brain of Admiral Cervera must be a thought, a design. But what ?

He had received a telegram dated from Cadiz stating that the *Huelva* was about to sail for Santiago.

The Cadiz squadron was waiting idly, daily expecting instructions from Cervera to sail in order to reinforce him. Yet from Cervera came no word. In his silent self-sufficiency there lurked a certain mystery, a hint of terror.

On the eighth evening of the blockade, the *Huelva* lay ten miles to the south by west of Santiago. Her engines almost stopped. She showed no lights. Immanuel Appadacca, wrapped from nose to heel in indiarubbers, ascended the broad stairway to her upper deck.

The captain of the vessel awaited him, and at once preceded him toward the fore-part of the ship. There a boat of strange shape, very slim and long, resembling a huge shark in hue and form, hung ready to be lowered. She already contained five invisible men, and near her, in the dim light, stood the lank figure of the priest. As Appadacca passed to the gleaming boat, Father Pedro lifted his right hand, bowed his head, and muttered an orison.

As soon as he had stepped on board the boat, Appadacca, too, disappeared. Rising from her flush deck a little forward of amidships was a small erection, an oblong box of steel, capable of containing a man. It was a tiny conning-tower. Within this Appadacca took his place.

The boat slid downward, and as soon as she touched the sea, flitted off, precisely in the manner of a fish, the water washing freely over her scudding deck.

She made toward the coast. In ten minutes she sighted the lights of the American warships, then proceeding to their deep-sea stations for the night ; in twenty she was right among them.

They were jerking white searchlight beams in wide erratic arcs all over the sea. Yet they did not detect the hurrying boat, passing sometimes within a cable-length of some forging ram ; for the fish-boat had put her fins into play, and sunk ten feet beneath the surface.

Even at this depth her speed was nine knots. Her motor was electric, supplied from storage batteries.

Every few minutes Appadacca rose from his dark course for an observation of distances and directions ; then immediately sank again.

He passed through the line of smaller craft near the harbour without having been observed. He entered the cañon. Here he rose. The forts had been forewarned of his passage.

In a few minutes he was on the deck of the *Vizcaya*, and was conducted to the Admiral's quarters, where he was awaited.

' I congratulate you upon your passage, señor,' said the Admiral, a plump and hale-looking man, with gray hair and cultured *bigote*.

Appadacca bowed.

' Our conference must necessarily be hurried,' he said. ' The *Huelva* lies yonder, and may find it necessary to show her heels to those people. Before then I should regain her. What, Admiral, are your intentions ?'

' They remain the same, señor, as those with which I came here originally. Santiago needed a third line of defence. I supply it.'

'It is, however, a rôle full of danger.'

'It may be, señor.'

'Fuller, perhaps, than you realize. It is the intention of the Americans to land some twenty thousand land-troops and marines with siege-guns; in such a case they will deliver a combined attack from sea and land, and, beyond doubt, block the harbour entrance by means of a sunken craft. In that case, you would be a prisoner, between two fires, and the end would be worse than destruction. It would be capture.'

'Never capture, señor. Be sure that I have sufficient dynamite on board my ships to blow them up.'

'Still, I have something better to suggest.'

'And that is——?'

'Not defence, but attack.'

'Willingly—if it be practicable. They, however, are twenty, and we are seven.'

'Eight—with the *Huelva*.'

'Ah, yes—that is so.'

'The suggestion is not primarily mine.'

'Whose then?'

'M. Hanotaux's.'

The Admiral's eyebrows lifted.

'And it is known and approved in Madrid?'

'Of that you may be certain.'

' And what is the direct motive ?'

' It is necessary to the friends of Spain that
Spain win at least one victory—the greater the
odds against her the better.'

' Then, señor, let us win it.   I, at least, am
ready.'

' Victory, however, is essential.   There must
be no failure here.   Before the attempt we
must have the certainty.'

' But how to get the certainty ?'

' By means of a little thought.   It is Thought,
in the end, and not metal guns which, in every
contest, prevails.   In that we all agree.   Yet
thought is almost invariably the last thing to
which men resort.'

' You have a scheme, señor ?'

' It is here,' said Appadacca, laying a pencilled
paper on the table.

The Admiral bent over it, and as he bent,
he smiled.

' This seems to me most admirable !' he said.
' Do you advocate to-night as the time ?'

' Why not at once ?'

A flush gradually overspread the Admiral's
face.   He rose and held out his hand to
Appadacca.   Appadacca had the trick of in-
spiring men.

# CHAPTER XVI.

## THE BATTLE.

For over two hours a continual bustle prevailed throughout the length and breadth of the Spanish ships. Collision mats were got ready; water-tight doors were closed; on the cleared decks preparations were made for rigging torpedo-nets. By the time all magazines were opened, and ammunition and projectiles got out, the ships lay with fires banked, and steam at a very few minutes' notice.

It was ten o'clock. Yonder, up the terraced hill, blinked Santiago through a thousand dim and sleepy eyes of light; silence was in the air, made deeper by the vague drone of the mosquito, the West Indian moscon, and the rare firefly. The air was black and hot. With every movement of the sea, luminous mists of phosphorescent lights danced and twisted and disappeared on its surface. The

noise of preparation on the ships died down,
and all was still. As for Appadacca, he was
reading, fifteen miles away, in the library of
the *Huelva*.

Then there was a quick panting of small
engines, a clank of chains. Captains of cruisers
and commanders of destroyers had returned
from a conference in the flagship. Boats were
swung up, and in ten minutes there was movement on the water.

The ships passed down the narrow channel,
the two destroyers leading. The unarmoured
*Reina Mercedes*, a rather lame duck, was left
in the harbour. At three hundred feet from
the entrance they were sighted by a passing
American torpedo-boat. When the foremost
of the Spaniards emerged, signal of their
coming had been flashed among the Americans.

The first object of Cervera was to escape
injury from this small flotilla, in order to engage
directly with the heavily-armoured ships under
the conditions as to sea-room and other things
arranged with Appadacca.

At the harbour mouth one of the destroyers
turned sharply to port, the other two to starboard; the four cruisers, the *Cristobal Colon*,
*Vizcaya*, *Almirante Oquendo*, and *Maria
Teresa*, steered south at only a cable-length's

interval, the *Vizcaya* leading. These were all ships of twenty knots, as modern as they were fast, with 12-inch armour-belts, plated decks, turrets firing two 28-cm. guns, with ten Hontoria 14-cm. guns, and eight 57-mm. quick-firers. The Americans had present no equally good combination of speed, power, and modernity.

At a thousand yards from the harbour entrance the cruisers had acquired a speed of twelve knots, while the position of the steam-cones told that they had power to spare. Every moment their rate accelerated. At nine hundred yards from the region of the Americans they were racing forward in line abreast.

Still no sound; the American ships are greatly spread out; three having gone racing eastward, four westward, to deal with the two destroyers, which else, with their high speed, will elude the blockade; only three are left in the centre of the American line to oppose the advancing cruisers.

The tactics of the Spaniards are to be silent for as long a time as possible, lest the big ships outside hear the rumour of the row. But suddenly, with one venomous exclamation, the stillness is over; the *Texas* has launched a needle of steel from her bow tube above the water-line. From her the centre of the advancing Spanish line is not more than two hundred yards away ; the torpedo plunges like a slim, athletic diver, and goes darting steadily, as if with headstrong design, straight for the ram of the *Cristobal Colon.* The sea is smooth, rolling in oily heaves. In another moment the torpedo is at the central armour-belt of the *Colon ;* it has touched, and runs, but as lightly as a piston glides in its cylinder ; there is contact without impact. In intense haste the needle glides sternward along the glassy metal, until it reaches the region of foam around the screws. The port-screw strikes it, and it utters its awful bark.

The stern of the *Colon* jumps a little upward, but without injury. The explosion is ten yards astern.

At that moment, along a line of five miles, the night breaks into smoky glare and bluster-ing, rolling hubbub.

But in the centre the row is so short as to resemble an exclamation. The four cruisers have broken the American line—the *Maria Teresa* with shattered fore-armoured tube, and the torpedo-boat *Texas* dipping by her broken bows.

Yonder, east and west, the American boats are crowding in pursuit of the two swift destroyers, training their lights and guns upon them as they rush at twenty-five knots through the whitening water. And there the sound of the battle congregates into two crowds of quick-cracking uproar, while from the outer sea the massive armaments of the Americans, pouring hurried masses of dense smoke from their funnels, come hasting in, in two lines ahead, at the noise of the fray.

That the four Spaniards can hope to live for five minutes in the presence of this accumulation of power seems like a madness. The *Massachusetts* is a 10,000-ton ship, with two barbettes, carrying 13-inch guns ; the *Iowa* is an 11,000-tonner, with four 45-ton guns. None of the Spaniards are over 9,000 tons, and they are four to ten.

On the weak side, however, is audacity, design, and the *Huelva*.

On board the *Huelva* there is a strange something swaying in the faint night-breeze near the second funnel. It is a great oat-shaped bag, made of twilled Lyons silk, coated within and without with gutta-percha, and it contains hydrogen gas, obtained by passing the steam from a small boiler through a furnace of coke and anthracite. Over it is a net, and attached to the net a hoop, and attached to the hoop a cubical wicker-work basket, capable of containing four men.

And since the four men who will now occupy it must necessarily—almost necessarily—die, the crew of the *Huelva* is drawn up on her upper deck, and her captain, passing before them, puts the case, and demands volunteers. Appadacca and the priest are standing on the poop. Some hundred right hands go up. The captain thinks a minute, and puts his hand on four shoulders.

At that moment the priest spoke, as if smitten by a sudden thought.

'But stop,' he said; 'we have a prisoner, señor. We may therefore save a life.'

Appadacca smiled, rather contemptuously.

'Does he, then, remain unconverted, Father?' he said.

'As unconverted as an ape. The man belongs to an impossible race.'

'But his life is a life also, is it not? Have we the right——?'

'A prisoner may be made to perform forced labour with justice. The man is joined to his idols.'

'Ah! I see—joined to his idols; therefore he must be—— Well, I naturally do not care what you do with this person, Father Pedro.

He is your prisoner, you know. If he no longer amuses you, destroy him by all means, if that is your whim.'

The priest at once went forward, and spoke some words to the captain. The captain descended into the cabin. As he did so, out, from hardly four miles away, broke the huge clamour of the meeting ships. The *Huelva* had need of haste.

The Americans were steaming directly north in two lines ahead at some eleven knots, the *Iowa* leading the port limb, the *Marblehead* the starboard. The Spaniards came south at fifteen knots, making an aggregate passing speed between ships of twenty-six knots, or nearly half a mile a minute. Yet in that swift by-rush of the ships—two of the Spaniards on the outside of the port limb of the Americans, and two on the outside of the starboard, and each ship belching a broadside within the space of four minutes of some 11,000 rounds of quick-firing and machine shot and shell—not a single unprotected man or gun on the Spanish ships was fit for further work. The crews in their military tops, as in the military tops of all the Americans, were no more ; and from the stern-works of the *Vizcaya* a wide, sparkling fume, thronged with ascending points of light, went

as a beacon through the night. The ships
turned, re-formed, and prepared to charge.

At that moment it was that the American
officers became aware of two things : First,
that one of the enemy's ships was flying ; and,
secondly, that an electric light was passing and
pouring, first upon one ship, then upon another,
downward from mid-air.

At this sight the heart of the boldest
quailed.

But it was to the running ship that Admiral
Sampson first turned his thought, in spite of
the impending doom above ; and out from the
*Brooklyn* at once went the trumpet-call, ordering two of the cruisers in that limb to join her
in the chase of the escaping ship. The speed
of the *Brooklyn* was twenty-one knots, at least
one knot faster than the speed of the fastest of
the Spanish cruisers.

The three ships, labouring under all steam,
went churning to the south-east, one of them
rattling as they did so the ribs of one of the
port Spaniards which came within effective
range.

But *which* of the Spanish cruisers was it
that they chased ? They did not know. And
they were hardly half a mile gone when
wonderment seized the rest of their fleet, for

there, certainly, returning to the charge, were
the four battered cruisers !

And now began to be revealed to all the
whole inwardness of the scheme of Appadacca ;
for yonder in the starboard line of the
Americans are only two ships left to fight
two, and in the port line, above the five, hangs
in the air a thing which will surely speak.

It is a thing which can make its way in the
air even in the face of a light breeze. It is
fitted with an electric light arrangement which
can throw its rays in a circle five feet wide
directly downward on the deck of a ship, and
its car is packed with dynamite shells, whose
steel casing contains liquid oxygen and blasting
gelatine.

Positively now, unless the small flotilla further
in shore speed at once to the aid of their ships
in deep water, it seems that there is no hope
for the concentrated fleet of America. But the
small flotilla have their work cut out in dealing
with the rushing destroyers, which are eluding
and attacking them in incalculable conflict.

Suddenly, just as the big bow-guns of the
ships begin to bark in the renewed attack,
there hoots a sound which drowns every other,
a sound at which the palefaced inhabitants of
Santiago, listening in horror to the thunders of

this hideous night, start with an intenser shiver.
One of the shells has dropped from that evil,
soaring thing directly above the engine-room
of the *Iowa ;* there resounds a series of heart-
appalling shocks, hurrying at last into a roaring
and raging rattle, as a spout of red and yellow
flames bursts high and far over the sea.   The
two fore-port magazines have been ignited,
and, as the ship lurches and dives, the thing
in the air sails onward a score of yards, and
manœuvres above the *Vixen*.

But what is the astonishment of Admiral
Sampson when he finds that the further he
chases, and the greater the agony of haste
with which he urges the *Brooklyn*, the further
seems to steal away the ship he follows.   When
he starts in pursuit, a barbette shot from his
bows bursts a hundred yards ahead of the
flying ship ; seven minutes afterwards she is
beyond effective range.

The Admiral, gazing abroad over the waters,
is puzzled, but determined.   He will follow her,
he says, to Hell—igoland; and as he goes tearing
on this wild-goose chase, the navy of America
behind him is being annihilated.

It is a question of minutes.

Suddenly, at a moment when the wide uproar of the spouting and thundering *Iowa* is

beginning to sink into a sullen muttering, a new, sharp sound breaks from the dark upon the Admiral's ear. It is a trumpet-call from a lightless ship travelling briskly in the opposite direction, two cable-lengths on his beam; and from the sonorous throat of brass came these words in vibrant distinctness to the Admiral's ear:

'Don't follow her, Sampson! it's the *Huelva!*'

The throat was the throat of the trumpet, but the words were the words of Dick P. Hocking.

The *Union* had arrived just in time to see the battle.

Straight onward she went, smoothly walking the water, dangerously near to the region of shrieking shell and white sea-thrash, and the quick jabbering of Nordenfeldts and Gardners, and balls of flying flame. At this time the Spaniards were for the second time turned outwards to the Americans, and the Americans for the second time shoreward to the Spaniards, all the Spaniards still afloat, and the odds four ships and the balloon to five ships.

But the balloon, cruising high up in darkness, except at the moment of action, when it cast its intense instantaneous fan of radiance, had an effective value of quite five or six other battleships.

13

At the moment when the slow, distant firing once more quickened into a sudden thronging outrage of hell-fire, bursting from both sides, dazing the brain and splitting the ear, the *Union* was perhaps two thousand yards to the southward of the southernmost American ship, and was still forging slowly ahead to the northward.    She had a searchlight playing, and Dick P. Hocking, in pyjamas, had his eyes at a night-glass on the poop.

His soul was in his gaze ; his lower jaw hung open a little.   Here, truly, was man's work—no child's-play—a thing which a man might do.   A kind of crooked smile distorted his gaping mouth.   It was a sight one might pay to be at—a thing a man of force and intelligence might set about himself, and take a pride in doing right well.   He looked, and he saw a flame burst from the forecastle of the *Cristobal Colon*, and go waving aft like a plume ; he saw the *Vixen* throw her humming screws into the air and her nose into the sea, as a duck when it dives ; and immediately afterwards he saw an intense light shoot downward upon the deck of the *Massachusetts*, and he made out the form of the balloon.   It was sailing on the land-breeze in the direction of the *Union*.

A shell broke into glare ninety feet from

THE MUZZLE POINTED UPWARD.

[*To face p.* 195.

Hocking, and sent a splinter into his aft sky-light.

Hocking hardly noticed. He had lifted a Winchester which had been leaning near, and had put it to his shoulder, the muzzle pointed upward.

He was in no hurry; he took his time. He cocked his right leg, and drew it in, and cocked it again. His left eye was shut tight. Then he pulled the trigger, and as he pulled it he muttered:

'You and your beastly jokes. . . !'

Like a creature which has received a deadly hurt, the balloon uttered a shriek, heard indistinctly by the men in her car. At that moment it dropped a shell, but it fell into the sea.

The car was seen to protrude its form into the region of smoky glare; then the hoop and strings; then the now lax and flaccid silken bag. Floating hopelessly, with languid abandonment, at the mercy of the wind, it drooped downward and outward. When the car touched the water, it was about two hundred yards from the *Union*. Her boat was out, ready to rescue.

The balloon floated quite steadily for a minute, then with an absolute suddenness disappeared.

At the same time the battle was over. The

three cruisers which had hurried after the
*Huelva* reappeared, long before they were
looked for by the Spaniards. The Spaniards
at the same moment saw the two sources of
hope upon which they relied cut off. The
*Huelva* was no longer pursued—the balloon
was in the water. Without hesitation the four
cruisers, one of them very low in the bows,
turned for the harbour at full speed, firing only
stern-guns. They found the passage clear, and
immediately on entering it were followed by the
destroyer *Terror*, which, with the *Pluton*, now
at the bottom, had accounted for five of the
American small craft.

The forts now opened fire to cover their
retreat, but, with the inefficiency of Spanish
forts, did no one any hurt. The *Massachusetts*,
growling her last growl as the last of the
Spaniards disappeared beyond a curve of the
cañon, withdrew sullenly to the outer sea.

Meantime Dick P. Hocking's abdomen was
in agitation, heaving with laughter. Up from
the boat sent to rescue the balloonists climbed
the Rev. Silas M. Petersen, streaming with
brine.

'Parson!' said Dick P. Hocking. 'This
can't be you, man! Why, I'm darned if it ain't
a case of Jonah and the whale's belly!'

'Guess you ain't far out there,' said Petersen ; 'though sharks are more in the line of business of these waters, I reckon.'

'But it *can't* be you! Is it you?'

'That's about what it comes to.'

'Then—you—are—the little parson for me!' cried Hocking, shaking his hand crazily ; 'that's about all I can say!'

# CHAPTER XVII.

## THE CHASE.

IT was necessary for Dick P. Hocking to return immediately to New York. During the night he received from Admiral Sampson a despatch for Washington, and set off eastward before break of day. He was perfectly serene, having no suspicion that his presence there was known to any enemy, or that he had been watched.

To his chagrin, the next morning at breakfast he received the news that the *Union* hardly had coal in her bunkers to take him to Tampa. It was either a question of returning to the fleet, or making for Cape Haytien. He was now a considerable distance out from Cuba, so he went about, having determined upon the other route homeward.

He coaled at Cape Haytien, and was not more than half an hour from the harbour when on the port bow he sighted the smoke of a big ship.

All on the *Union* were very much on the *qui vive ;* an eager look-out was kept. The rate of approach of the other vessel was phenomenal ; one seemed able to see her growth on the horizon. Before the *Union* herself could have been visible to the other, it was definitely made out that the other was the *Huelva.*

And now Dick P. Hocking had searchings of heart. He had felt the keenness of Appadacca's sting, and for various reasons, at this precise juncture, he was averse to feeling it again.

He called a conference in the cabin—himself, Petersen, the captain. Petersen said that, in his opinion, the *Huelva* had seen the *Union* on the night of the battle, and surmised the share which the small vessel had had in the determining of events. He would not be surprised, he said, to find in her master the petty spite of a woman. The *Huelva* was seeking the *Union.*

' Then what to do ?' queried Hocking.

What *not* to do Petersen knew. They must not think for that day of the ordinary route to Tampa. The *Huelva* would be upon them before nightfall; they must pursue, while still unobserved, their eastward course.

So eastward the *Union* went.

At Savanna, Hocking heard by telegram from an agent in Cape Haytien that a fishing-boat of the port had been stopped by the *Huelva*, which had demanded news of the *Union*. The boat had given it. The *Huelva* was therefore on her way eastward in search of the *Union*.

Then again there was conference, anxious heads laid together. Petersen lived studying the map. He gave his voice, and Hocking agreed, for proceeding still eastward, to find perhaps a hiding-place among the islands of the Lesser Antilles. When the *Huelva* shot further eastward than they, then they would return on their westward course.

For three days the *Union* neither heard of nor saw the *Huelva;* she prepared to retrace her long détour. They were seven miles to the windward of the island of Nevis when, in a new laying-together of heads, this step was agreed upon at an early hour of a bright tropical morning.

However, they had hardly come to this decision when there was commotion on deck, a series of calls from bow to stern, and all

the signs of that excitement among sailors
when the monotonous deep brings forth a
sensation.

Dick P. Hocking and Silas M. Petersen ran
at once above.

It was towards the south-east end of Nevis,
on the windward side of the island.

Hocking, Petersen, and the captain of the
*Union* put glasses to their eyes, turned to the
north-west, and mused. The pennant of smoke
in the distance acquired distinctness; it grew
rapidly.

'Say,' said Dick P. Hocking, 'is that thing
there the *Huelva*? Yes or no?'

The Rev. Petersen slowly lowered his glasses,
and he said: 'Guess it is, this time.'

A sound of vexed impatience came from
Hocking's lips.

'Darn the thing!' he said. 'Isn't anything
to be done, man? I'm not over keen on
falling into that liverless Spaniard's hands
right now, either.'

Petersen did not answer. He stood thinking
a minute; then he ran towards the chart-
room.

In less than two minutes he reappeared.

'Guess there's a chance,' he said. 'What's
your very best speed, captain?'

And as he looked he groaned, and the heavy lids of his eyes drooped lower in a sulky frown. But no one could have told by regarding the man that within he was all a-tingle with apprehension.

The bell went clang-clang, then again after two seconds clang-clang: four bells in the forenoon watch. The *Huelva* was ten miles astern. Her hull now was visible through the glasses.

But now, too, the azure mirage which had been Redonda began to be no longer azure, nor a mirage; streaky opal zigzags of rock lined its face, and one saw that it was not a cloud, but solid land.

The Rev. Silas M. Petersen walked the bridge; his hands trembled with eagerness. Would he not be too late? The waving pennant of the *Huelva's* smoke was like a brag of invincible speed. The captain ran to the engine-room stair, and, calling the chief engineer half-way up, cried:

'For Heaven's sake, get every inch you can out of her!'

The sea whitened round the toiling *Union*. The *Huelva* stretched like a greyhound bent upon a leveret.

The island towards which they were hasting

was a mere rock, rising with craggy sides
from the water, conical in shape, and unin-
habited, save by boobies, and three men who
live on its summit for the purpose of collecting
the guano of the innumerable sea-fowl which
haunt its shrubless sea-wall. The three men
are lifted and lowered from and to the sea by
a basket-and-crane arrangement high up on
the face of the rock. From the summit a view
(which the present writer has twice enjoyed) is
obtained for many a mile over the sea as far as
the coasts of Nevis to the north and Montserrat
to the south.

By the time the ravines and indentations of
the rock had come to seem to the *Union* near
and real, the *Huelva* was five miles astern.
The great ship sent up the single signal in the
common code :

' Stop !'

The *Union* kept on her way.

There was a minute's silence of fear and
awful expectancy, and at the end of it one of
the nine-inch fore-barbette guns of the *Huelva*
sent out a rush of redness. Then came a shell
travelling in silent swiftness along the water ;
a ball shot with extraordinary precision from
a distance usually beyond effective range,
making right in the wake of the *Union*, bound

without fail for her poop.   Certainly the crew
of the *Huelva* had among them at least one
perfect marksman.

But the shot, fired too far off, dived into a
wave twenty yards astern of the *Union*.   The
rock was two miles ahead of her.

Dick P. Hocking, standing now with Petersen on the bridge, said :

' Parson, this time, I reckon——'

' They'd better look lively about it, then,'
answered Petersen.   ' They've got exactly
seven minutes and a half to do their work in.
If they linger, they'll lose the deal.'

' But how, man —— ?'

' Wait—you'll see.'

The *Huelva* was evidently reserving her
next shot for closer quarters.   It was quite
four minutes before it left her bows.   She
was then within four miles astern of the
*Union*.

And the shell came with the same appalling
precision of aim, crying that peculiar busy
shriek of large shrapnel fired over water.   It
was clearly meant to annihilate the screws and
rudder of the *Union*, and it struck.

At the moment of impact, however, the
*Union* was on the point of mounting a wave,
her bows up, her stern low ; the shell caught

the extremity of her upper stern-works, and sent the woodwork spouting and hovering sixty feet into air, like a scattered group of black sea-birds.

That was all. When the burst of uproar was over, the flash and smoke out of the eyes, and the wreckage a hundred yards astern, it was seen that rudder, steering-gear, and screws remained intact.

'Now, at last, I guess we're safe,' said Petersen.

'Believe me, parson, I don't understand you!' cried Hocking. 'How safe?'

'Well, they can't have that gun ready for another shot within four minutes, I reckon; and unless they fire upon us from their broadside, or from a military-top, they'll find us under cover next round sure enough.'

'Under cover? Where?'

'Behind the rock.'

'But they'll come behind, too, I guess?'

'Then we'll be on another side when they do.'

'But——'

'That's so.'

'Yes; but they are miles faster than we.'

'Not in dodging round that rock, sir.'

'Anywhere.'

'But not there.'

'Why not ?'

'Because the inner of two circles is the smaller, any day. We can get in nearer than they—so the chart says, and so the captain ˋsays.'

Hocking's eyes opened wide, and his mouth.

'Well, I'm darned if I don't think you're right!' he cried after half a minute, and he shook Petersen's hand in a grip that meant many things.

As he did so Petersen clutched him, cried, 'Look out!' and skulked behind the railing. A rain of machine-gun shot fell ripping and smashing upon the quarter-deck.

'Hard down!' cried the captain at the same moment.

They were at the rock. In perhaps half a minute the *Huelva* was hidden from the *Union* by a bluff. The small ship was not two cable-lengths from the shore.

Even within few yards of the narrow strip of sand the water is deep ; but the bottom shelves very gradually outward, so that for a considerable distance to sea the rock is unapproachable by such a ship as the *Huelva*, with draught of twenty-five feet. In order to steam round the rock, it was therefore necessary for her to traverse a distance some three times greater than that necessary for the *Union*, and her speed was not nearly three times greater. When the *Union* found herself under shelter she slackened speed.

Presently the bow of the *Huelva* was seen, far out, peeping round the brow of a headland, but by the time her whole length emerged the *Union* had disappeared behind a curve of land. They went steaming round the rock, hiding and seeking.

And all the length of that tropical day they resembled two persons dodging round a table. Sometimes the *Huelva* slackened speed and waited; and presently there, stealing forward far within, would come the *Union;* and before a volley could leave the broadside of the great yacht the other had turned and disappeared. Sometimes, again, the *Huelva* would fly in circular career with all the power of her travailing engines, but always the smaller ship could beat her in the revolution of the rock.

Moreover, the *Union* had a three-pounder on board with which she could readily have sunk a boarding-boat. But no such attempt was made.

It was towards one bell, second dog-watch,

14

when the sun's lower rim had touched the horizon, that the *Huelva* turned her bows finally away.

And as she did so the *Union* for a minute or two stood boldly out, and on her main stood arrayed in signal-flags these words :

' Next time *I* will do the chasing.'

# CHAPTER XVIII.

### THE 'JANE RICHARDSON.'

THE *Union* was not more anxious to be out of her imprisonment round Redonda and to be away than was the *Huelva*.

One went toward the north and east, the other toward the north and west. The man whom Appadacca was anxious above all others to see was M. Hanotaux; the man whom Hocking was bent upon seeing was Cramp, of Philadelphia.

He determined that Immanuel Appadacca had been leading him a dance long enough. He had begun it seven years before, and he was doing it still, with his beastly jokes.

Hocking spent three extremely active days at New York, transacting a world of business connected with the general running of his house. What kept him back longest was the getting of the *Jane Richardson* to sea.

14—2

She was a 5,000 - ton steamer, rather old, barque-rigged—for the most part a Rio and Liverpool trader—one of the makers of the house of Hocking. She was off now to Rio, and she had on board three hundred thousand pounds in gold specie. On the third day Dick P. Hocking saw her drop down the harbour past Fort Wandsworth into the Narrows. And at once, with Petersen, who meanwhile had preached a thrilling discourse at Brooklyn on the horrors of war (by an eye-witness), he set off for Philadelphia.

He knew that there was something there for him to see. What there was for him to see was two boats lying quietly in the Inner Dock —black, ugly things, low in the water, with the curve of a ram indicated at the water-line ; small craft, one a hundred and forty feet long, one two hundred and twenty ; and within one three tubes, and within the other, five. Besides these, there is a third on the stocks — the biggest of the three—a cross between a torpedo-boat and a destroyer. A yard from the rudder of the first is painted on her side the large white figure 1 ; in a similar place on the second the figure 2 ; on the third the figure 3 : 1 and 2 have already had trial-trips, and the speed of 1 is twenty-five, and of 2 twenty-eight ; the speed of 3 is estimated at thirty-three, her indicated horse-power being four thousand eight hundred.

And on the dock-quay stood Dick P. Hocking, right hand in pocket, left behind his back, leg projected, with slanting, contemplative head. He looked up at the short mast with the cross-tree, and his eye followed it to the hull ; and from the low stern to the high stem his eye travelled along the lengthy rake of beam. And on his left Petersen stood, and looked with slanting head ; and on his right, Cramp, with slanting head.

Twenty men, leaning over the side of No. 1, and twenty-three over the side of No. 2, got a signal from Cramp, and understood who it was that was inspecting them ; and they sent up a cheer.

And Hocking said :

' That's about something like what I wanted. And No. 3—I request to know the earliest date at which she can be put to sea ?'

' Say Thursday,' said Cramp—' four days from now.'

' Coal and everything ?'

' Fifty-five tons of it.'

As they were leaving the yards, a telegram was placed in the hand of Dick P. Hocking.

It came from the captain of the *Jane Richardson*, which had put in by order at Charleston. It was a rather lengthy communication ; it ended by saying :

'Strange man came on board during my absence in port, and got from first officer all information as to cargo, etc., under false pretences, apparently.    Guess from description disguised Spaniard.    Apprehend danger, perhaps groundlessly.'

Dick P. Hocking handed the telegram first to Petersen, and then to Mr. Cramp.

'Guess that ship could do with a bit of convoying,' he muttered with a nod.

And Petersen nodded, too, and Cramp was serious.

'You both look like agreeing with me,' said Hocking.

'It has that appearance,' assented Cramp.

'Then, what you've got to do is to make those four days three, or even two, if human nature can screw itself up to it.'

Cramp speculated upon the ground.

'Can't be done, sir !' he said with decision.

'It can, if I make it worth your while ; and I will.    Three days at the outside, and there's fifteen thousand dollars over and above the contract. Why, man, a million and a half in solid gold is at stake here!'

'Well, I might shake hands on three days, perhaps ; but it's a risk, I guess. As it is, no dockyard on this earth ever turned out ships at the rate we've run these. But I can only try, that's all.'

So they went forth, and drank champagne : and as they were drinking, Immanuel Appadacca, on the other side of the ocean, was drawing on his gloves at a window in the salon of his suite in the Hôtel de l'Athenée, Paris.

Behind him sat Josef Campos, nervously turning the leaves of the *Figaro*. He turned them to the end, and began again from the beginning. He wanted to say something which he found it hard to say.

Appadacca turned to go. He bowed as he passed Campos, with a 'Buenos dias, caballero.'

Campos coughed.

'Am I wrong in thinking that you have something to communicate ?' said Appadacca, stopping.

'Señor, we are—*very*—pressed for money,' answered Campos, coming straight to the point.

Appadacca laughed.

'Excuse my levity, Señor Campos,' he said,

'but you said the words with *such* an air of seriousness !'

'But—is it not, then, serious, señor ?'

'Is it ? It may be. I never gave the matter a thought. But I will ; you may rely upon me.'

'Thank you, señor.'

'Meantime, the time you choose is inopportune for the discussion of a matter of that sort. I cannot wait ; I am about to meet the French Minister. Pray refer to the subject again. Good-day.'

His close brougham was at the door. He drove south-westward to the Foreign Office, where he was awaited. He was soon closeted with M. Hanotaux.

Hanotaux continually stroked his straggling imperial, and there was rather an underlook in his eyes as the conference proceeded.

'It is necessary for me, monsieur,' Appadacca said, speaking French, 'to know how far and how near is the intervention of Europe in this war, before I can take further steps.'

'The intervention, I fear, is where it was, señor,' said M. Hanotaux. 'You know of that natural condition of very cold water in a glass or cup : the least shake of the vessel will make it shudder into solid ice, but in the absence of the shake, it remains liquid an indefinite time.'

' The naval affair at Santiago, and the loss of the Americans therein, does not, then, affect the European situation ?'

' It was *nearly* a great victory, señor,' said Hanotaux with a bow. 'Certainly, it was organized with consummate skill; but the results, I must say, have not struck Europe with the vividness which your generalship richly deserves.'

' You compliment me too much, monsieur. The affair was entered upon at your suggestion. Is another attempt necessary ?'

' It would be difficult now, señor.'

' Nothing is difficult, monsieur.'

' Still, there are other points upon which the activities of the friends of Spain might at this moment be more profitably directed.'

' And those are ?'

' Firstly and chiefly, the prevention of the invasion of Cuba by land-troops—or, at least, the retardation.'

' And why, monsieur ?'

' Because—because——.   I tell you that there's not a single State in Europe which is not secretly and strongly on the right side. Germany, it is already known in diplomatic

circles, is prepared to interfere—actively, if
need be, if only in Manila.   Of France and
Russia, of Italy and Austria, you have no
doubt.   Even in England, I assure you, the
middle and upper classes favour Spain.   It is
only the rabble and the base press of that
country which have had the bad taste to range
themselves on the queer side.   As for Germany,
well, Italy, of course, is her ally, and Italy is
the cousin of Spain.   You may be sure that
Italy, if it be suggested to her, will do all the
spurring of Germany which may be necessary ;
in fact, none is necessary.   But I say this :
Spain must not make it too difficult for her
friends ; she must not show herself incompetent.
She must not permit herself to be invaded—at
least, not just yet.'

'You have now told me the why, monsieur,'
said Appadacca, 'but as to the how?   The
invasion of Cuba is regarded as more or less
inevitable.'

'It may, however, be retarded, till the friends
of Spain decide together upon their course.'

'And how?'

'By means of a real phantom fleet.'

'Ah?   Pray be more explicit.'

'You know how many phantom Spanish fleets
have lately been seen near the coasts of America

and in other parts of the world. Suppose, immediately before the embarkation of American
troops for Cuba, a well-authenticated phantom
fleet be seen in the distance. Since the troops
must necessarily be unconvoyed for lack of
warships, there I think you would have a
perfectly sure method of delaying the embarkation for some considerable time.'

' But "well - authenticated "?' said Appadacca.

' Yes ; hence I say " a *real* phantom fleet."
The ships must really be seen by perfectly
trustworthy witnesses, for the effect of a mere
report would simply be nil. Meantime, while
the mysterious fleet was being seen, the Spanish
Premier might persistently declare the Spanish
ships to be at Cadiz—which would be perfectly
true, but which would be at once supposed
in America to be perfectly false. The mysterious fleet would thus be infallibly assumed to be
Spanish.'

' Precisely, monsieur. But since this phantom
fleet is, as you say, to be composed of real
ships—and since the Spanish fleet at Cadiz is
unready to put to sea—where, think you, is
Spain to procure this phantom fleet ?'

' Ah, that is the business of Spain ; I merely
make the suggestion,' said M. Hanotaux,

stroking his *barbiche*, his mouth a little open. ' I might also make this further suggestion, that such a thing as the *borrowing* of a fleet has been more than once known, señor.'

With such delicacy had the suggestion been led up to, that Appadacca was now expecting it, and showed no surprise.

' If we must borrow, monsieur,' he said with a bow, ' it is surely from France that we would choose to borrow.'

' And if France is to be a lender, señor, it is surely to Spain, above all, that she would choose to lend.'

The two men were all bows and smiles.

'We, however,' said M. Hanotaux, 'are in this unfortunate position, that the present Government is, from hour to hour, uncertain of its tenure of office. Very soon, in fact, it is certain that a crisis will come ; M. Méline will resign ; a new Ministry will be formed. Nor am I sure that I shall then be asked to retain my portfolio of foreign affairs ; and the Minister of Marine is in the same predicament.'

' I follow you closely, monsieur.'

' It results from those facts that we must be in a position at any moment to give an account of our stewardship.  The cost of an expedition of French ships on a service not French would therefore necessarily be defrayed by the nation benefited. The Ministre de la Marine assures me that the cost on the whole, including loss of home-service and expenditure, would amount to six hundred thousand francs.'

' You will not, pray, be at all concerned as to that, monsieur,' said Appadacca. ' I, personally, undertake to be responsible for the amount, and will refund it as soon as ever it becomes due, tendering you, in addition, the most earnest, the most profound thanks of my country.'

Shortly after this the interview closed. Appadacca had no sooner reached his hotel than a telegram, dated Rome, was handed him. It was from the priest, Don Pedro, who had been sent first to Turin, to conduct negotiations with the Canon, and thence to the Vatican, with which he had been in correspondence through the Pope's Vicar-General. Father Pedro wired in cipher :

' Interview with Cardinal Parocchi quite successful. Germany certain. No cross-currents. Vatican and Crown pull together here. Immediately necessary for what you surmise—nine hundred thousand lires.'

Appadacca, still gloved, read the telegram

standing. To Campos sitting in the balcony he threw it.

'There, señor,' he said, 'is yet a further call upon your resources. Will you be also good enough to add to the nine hundred thousand lires, say, six hundred thousand francs, which will be due from you to the French Government within, let us guess, a week.'

Appadacca threw down his hat, and began to draw off his gloves. Campos came before him, standing with pallid, agitated face.

'Señor!' he said, 'is it that you persist in mocking me after my long service? or do you assume the rôle of the *ingénu* out of mere merriment?'

Appadacca with a quick movement confronted him, surprised.

'What do you mean?' he asked.

'To be quite frank, señor,' said Campos, 'it is rather a question with me how to pay our current expenses, our hotel and travelling bills, than the meeting of monstrous Governmental demands such as you mention. To myself, at least, I seem to deserve some sympathy from a faithfully-served master.'

'And I give it you, señor,' said Appadacca. 'I think, however, that I remember reproving you, and this very day, for taking with so ponderous an air what cannot be a matter of supreme importance.'

As he spoke a footman entered with a telegram. Appadacca glanced through it, and flung it to Campos, saying carelessly as he left the room :

' See, señor, how Providence opens for you interesting methods of repairing your collapsed commissariat. I will even assist you in the matter.'

The telegram was from Charleston, and came from one Fernandez.

It described the cargo of the *Jane Richardson*, the sum she carried in specie, her destination, hour of sailing, course. Her owners, it said, were the house of Richard P. Hocking, of New York.

# CHAPTER XIX.

## THE PRIZE.

APPADACCA left Paris hurriedly that night, directing his course toward Madrid, where he arrived incognito, and at once made his way to the house of Señor Sagasta.

The interview was hurried, Appadacca merely indicating the prominent, if secret, part he was being called upon to play in directing the destinies of the country — the sacrifices he made in wealth and, what to him was far more, in time. He said quietly, but in a tone which implied the will of steel, that when the right hour came, and the need for his open guidance, he would not fail to present himself as the leader of the leaderless country ; and, for so long a time as he chose, would expect to be recognised as such by whosoever in the land was unwilling to feel the hand of iron beneath the velvet palm.

And at once, when he was certain that he was well understood, off he set by special train for the Bay of Algeciras, wherein lay his well-loved ship.

Here he met Campos and the priest.

He was intensely eager to join her, to be away. In spite of a certain nonchalance which he affected as to all mundane matters, such as money, not only to Joseph Campos, but even to himself, he was in reality of a perfectly practical nature. His calculations had the exactness of a ready-reckoner, and many a time the hard, close-seeing eye of Dick P. Hocking had found the eye of Appadacca a mile the shrewder.

He calculated in the luxury of his library the means of catching the *Jane Richardson* with all the astuteness and the caution of an old miser.

And he did not fail.

By the time the *Jane* was at the Bahamas, the *Huelva* had reached the latitude of the Canaries. And the two ships were converging sharply in a southerly direction, when Dick P. Hocking, commanding his flotilla of three, set out from Philadelphia; and with him, borne in No. 3, was the Rev. Silas M. Petersen.

The object of Hocking was twofold. It

was, in the first place, to convoy the *Jane Richardson;* in the second, to see the *Huelva* in the air to the dance of torpedo-music. But in order to see her in the air, it was necessary first to see her; and the sea is wide. He expected to have a search of at least some weeks.

Meanwhile, with eager pump of the mighty engines in his small craft, he pushed on south in search of the *Jane,* his great bulk wrapped in oilskins, and he for the first time learning what a joy and a misery lay in ranging the ocean in a tearing torpedo-boat.

But with wondrous quick adaptability he became quite a sailor, growing in few days to tolerate the fearful vibratory heave of those toiling and swaying flanks.

He feared danger from some Spanish ship-of-war, without precisely thinking of the *Huelva,* and on without pause he drove. As for Petersen, he had the air of one born in a destroyer.

When the *Jane* was at Trinidad, the *Huelva* was in the longitude of Cayenne, not six hundred knots from her, and Hocking's flotilla was near St. Kitts. He knew that the *Jane* would put in at Port of Spain, so from the Lesser Antilles he wired her not to leave that English port until he joined her.

But the message was just too late ; the *Jane* was gone.

And the next day at three p.m. she sighted the *Huelva* on her port quarter, and was in turn sighted by the *Huelva*, which rapidly drew near.

# CHAPTER XX.

## THE BEGINNING OF THE END.

AT the moment when the ships came within each other's ken, each appeared like a tiny tail of gray only just deeper than the gray of the sky on the far horizon.

The *Jane* was steering about south-east, the *Huelva* south-west.

The captain and first officer of the *Jane* held steady glasses to their eyes on the bridge, and the mere speed with which that brush of gray afar grew darker upon the vision was enough to spur suspicious alarm.

Presently the captain growled.

'What do you make of her?' he asked.

The first officer shrugged his shoulders.

'What *I* say,' said the captain, 'is that she is after us, and a foreigner. That's enough for me. I have three hundred thousand sterling on board this ship. Here's to run for it.'

'Not much good, apparently,' answered the first officer, 'by the way she's raging along there. What a devil of a speed!'

'There's night,' said the captain, 'and luck —confound her!'

And he rushed to the communications, and trilled down to the engine-room, 'Full speed ahead!' At the same time the *Jane's* bows swung round eight points to starboard.

And she had hardly done so when the *Huelva*, certain now that she had found what she sought, bounded, like a courser at the spur, under the yet more quickened travail of her engines.

But the captain of the great yacht walked his bridge with too eager a step; his hands in his pockets, his brows knit. His dark countenance was anxious.

He did not expect—he was not prepared for —a long chase. Half an hour before, an ominous message had come to him from the engine-room. He continually dived his head inside a door, and looked at the clock.

The *Huelva* ordinarily consumed about a ton of coal in six knots; but the three thousand five hundred odd miles which she had traversed since leaving Algeciras on this money-hunting voyage had been performed at enormous speed, with heavy smoke continually pouring from her funnels ; nor, owing to the urgency of her master, were her bunkers quite full at the moment of departure.

The chase had lasted half an hour, the two hulls being now clearly visible to each other, when the captain of the *Huelva* groaned.  His eye had long been haunting some dark clouds on the southern horizon, and with that hurry of preparation characteristic of the sudden, passionate tempests of the West Indies, these now rose, and went ranging in haste across the sky, while half a dozen darts of rain fell upon the ship.

Her captain took pen, ink, and paper, and, in his imperfect handwriting, stated the case : Should he continue the chase ?  The chief engineer had reported that there were not more than forty tons of coal in the bunkers.  In ten minutes all the sea and sky would be wrapped in midnight ; the other ship, if she knew her business, would be certain to dodge.  Should he fire now, though they were well beyond effective range ?  Should he cease the chase till after coaling in Trinidad ?  He was at a loss.

He sent the note below.  It passed through five hands, and at length reached the deep-shaded library and the eyes of Appadacca.

Appadacca, at this foreboding news, started. The *Jane* was absolutely necessary to him. The money-claims upon him, both in France and Italy, were pressing. He wrote on the back of the sheet, after a full minute's deep meditation :

'Continue chase. Report to me in ten minutes.'

As the captain above read these words, suddenly the two ships were hid from each other. A passion of wind and water swept down upon the sea, shutting the ships in an isolation of storm and stinging white rain. The sky was quite black. And at once, with the first rush of the wheeling gloom, the *Jane's* bows turned four more points to starboard. She was running straight back for the southern end of Trinidad.

That she would dodge in the darkness, the captain of the *Huelva* well knew ; but he calculated that she would dodge in the most divergent direction, and so turned his bows about north, while in reality the *Jane* was heading nearly east.

In half an hour the storm cleared somewhat, and then the two ships had so far diverged as to be invisible. The *Huelva* was running with a line of Trinidad hills showing faintly on her port bows; the *Jane* was lapsing from the heaving outer sea into the absolutely smooth water of the Gulf of Paria.

Trinidad approaches the mainland of South America closely at two points: at a south channel called the Serpent's Mouth, and at a north called the Dragon's Mouth; between these and the mainland and the eastern coast of the island lies the placid gulf.

While the *Jane* was passing north into the Serpent's Mouth, Dick P. Hocking's flotilla of three was passing south into the Dragon's Mouth.

The *Huelva* was scouring the sea for the *Jane*, and the three torpedo-boats were scouring the sea for the *Huelva* and the *Jane*. And while the *Jane* and the three boats were making along the east coast, one north, the others south, the *Huelva* was making along the west coast, northward.

As the sun, a marred blotch, was disappearing for the day, the chief engineer of the *Huelva* sent up formal notice that he had only twenty-eight tons of coal in his bunkers. The captain rang half-speed.

At this time the flotilla of three were at anchor in Port of Spain. There the intelligence

was received that the *Jane* had gone on southward through the Serpent's Mouth ; so, after
surrounding his craft with lighters, which worked
through the night, and taking in about seventy
tons of coal, Hocking, while it was yet dark,
towards morning, set out to continue his southward search.

And because the *Jane*, fearing that the
*Huelva* might be tracking her in the dark, had
put out all external lights, the three boats which
sought her passed her at an interval of two
knots on their starboard side toward the south
end of the island, they faring south, she north :
her object being to pass through the north
channel, and then resume her course, on the
chance of eluding the *Huelva* by the long dodge.

By ten o'clock a.m. she was out in the rough
sea once more. The storm had lasted through
the night with lulls and outbursts. The morning on the open sea was murky and bleak ; it
was as though the wind was visible and shut
off the distance. Five miles away, unseen, the
*Huelva* was cruising slowly in search of the
*Jane*.

Something like despair reigned on board the
great ship. She had steamed very slowly
through the night, yet things looked ugly. At
last the captain sent down word that he had

only sufficient coal to take him to Port of
Spain.

Then only Appadacca yielded. The ship
turned her bows southward, and in ten minutes
sighted the *Jane*, now so near as to be within
range of small gunshot. She was recognised,
and at once the *Huelva*, with glad haste, sent
her bark across the water.

The *Jane* instantly turned tail, and as she
turned became the target for some three
hundred rounds, which shattered the sea-
surface all about her into a frothing chaos,
and shivered her bulwarks. Also a wide smoke
arose from her stern-works. And at once she
slowed, and waited.

The *Huelva* steamed near and put out a
boat. Her captain and five men went on
board the *Jane*; there were confabulations,
gesticulations, oaths, on the bridge ; but within
a quarter of an hour the boat returned with the
specie stored in *coffre-forts*.

Things looked well now on board the big
ship. But we are never certain for what to
thank the gods, since in their good is ill, and in
their ill good. The *Jane* was the bad genius
of the *Huelva*. She made Appadacca decide
not to put into Trinidad for coal. In the
bunkers of the *Jane* was plenty.

But the process of transhipment was bitterly slow, and Dick P. Hocking's flotilla, though steering at the moment of capture in an opposite direction, was swift. All the boats of both ships were employed in the work; but the sea ran high, and the *Huelva* avoided frequenting the smooth channel of the Gulf with the *Jane* bearing witness beside her. The slow work went on. A boat was swamped, another broke her bows against the *Jane's* side; two of the *Jane's* had been powdered by four-inch shell; all were more or less small. So passed the day; at night, with such a sea, it was impossible to work. A prize-crew was stationed on board the *Jane*. The next morning the slow labour recommenced.

The object of the *Huelva* was to get in merely sufficient to take her to Grenada or one of the near islands; in the last resort, Martinique. The loose way in which the regulations as to contraband of war had been fulfilled in the West Indies since the outbreak of hostilities left no reason for doubt that coal would be obtained in plenty. Moreover, the *Huelva's* letters of marque did not make her strictly a combatant.

Slowly rose the tale of tons: sixteen, eighteen, twenty, enough to take her to Grenada; not half enough to take her to Martinique. It was decided to ride through another night, get in thirty tons, and start.

All this time the two ships lay rather out of the route from Barbadoes, to the east of Macaripe, with the bold profile of mountainous Trinidad showing like some vague and distant mist.

And once again, as the sun rose upon a less fierce and boisterous sea, the flotilla of boats went plying with their little loads. The *Huelva* had stowed just twenty-three tons, when her captain put down a glass, and rushing to the telephone, whistled. He said :

' I notice three steam-craft from the south-east making straight this way.'

' What are they ?' asked Appadacca.

' I will tell you in three or four minutes. They seem small, but strange somehow. Shall——'

' Get up steam.'

In six minutes the captain of the *Huelva* made out that the three boats were war vessels, and that they carried the American flag.

The men working in the boats scurried at the call of the siren on board their own ship. There was confusion, pattering of feet, crews organizing themselves to places, the voice of the captain, and the cry of electric bells. The *Huelva's* lofty bows walked round to northward, holes here and there gushed trickles into the sea, puffed whiffs into the air, while vast foam-billows rose and rolled before the advancing ram, as the ship began to foot the deep. And on in her wake came the three torpedo-boats.

They had proceeded south and east to a point which, according to the news received at Trinidad, it was certain that the *Jane* could not yet have reached. They concluded, there-fore, that they had passed her. They turned back to cruise in search, and off Point Baja fell in with a barque which had passed the *Jane* toward morning the day after her first *rencontre* with the *Huelva;* the *Jane* was then steering northward in her flight.

If the *Jane* were doing anything so un-accountable as to be sailing *northward*, then it could only be that she was being chased. So reasoned Hocking and Petersen, and at once they set off northward, also along the eastern Trinidad coast.

And as soon as ever their glasses turned upon the *Jane*, she was recognised by them, and near her unmistakably lay the *Huelva*.

And as the *Huelva* turned and steamed away, one of the fleet of three hoisted four flags, and the three smothered themselves and the sea in a coverlet of smoke.

And leaving the *Jane* there with a message from Hocking to go on to Port of Spain, the four passed on northward, the foremost seven or eight knots from the hindermost.

# CHAPTER XXI.

## THE CHASE.

DICK P. HOCKING had said that the next time *he* would do the chasing, and he was doing it. Yet he might have sought the *Huelva* all over the broad face of the sea and never have found her; but the *Jane* was the decoy-bird which had revealed her.

He had no knowledge of the *Huelva's* fatal lack of coal. He simply dared with the three comparatively tiny craft he commanded to oppose himself to that tremendous power which he followed.

Torpedo-boat against battleship; the novel, the original, against old use-and-wont; Saxon against Latin.

He followed.

His boats were literally robed and drowned in white from stem to stern, their ribs rocking

in horrible, heaving, vibratory fits. Like a
creaky chair too frail for the weight that
bestrides and rocks it, so these creaked and
rocked at the throbs and impulse of their
pumping - engines. They were all of very
high speed, and within ten minutes it was
clear that they gained upon the *Huelva*,
till the captain of the *Huelva* himself noticed
it, whereupon she quickened her run to the
utmost, and stole away somewhat from the
boats.

But at a disastrous cost. She could do a
good pace under sail alone, but now she was
heading in the teeth of the prevailing West
Indian wind, the north - east. There was,
therefore, no question of sail ; she depended
solely upon steam, having twenty odd tons of
coal.

Appadacca knew that he was being chased
by ships carrying the American flag ; he knew
his lack of coal ; but he continued in the
deep recesses of that part of the ship which
formed his sanctuary, preoccupied with matters
as trivial as possible. During the first half-
hour a dark-hued violin was at his shoulder,
and he was uttering, in the dreamiest slow under-
tone, that resembled a sigh, one of Bach's
fugitive fancies ; then, his mood changing,

he leapt up, drew a drawer from a cabinet, and laid before him a collection of stones, the delicate wine - tone of amethyst, gross copper-green of augite, with sardius, and chrysoberyl, and thulite, and that blue-stone with which the denizens of Ararat ward off dropsy. He held them one by one in tenuous fingers beneath the rosy light of a central lamp, searching the secret of their hues. He set about arranging them in sets.

Behind him ploughed the ugly snouts of Dick P. Hocking's torpedo-boats with steady forge.

The Latin was playing prettily ; the Saxon was working vulgarly.

It was Appadacca himself who had given the order to fly. Fear was not in his nature ; he was pride incarnate. He made the quick resolve, on learning that he was pursued, to seek out these particular boats on the first possible occasion, and ruthlessly batter them from the face of the sea. But for the moment he had pressing engagements in Europe. Till they were fulfilled he shunned a conflict.

And Hocking, clinging to a davit of No. 3 near the one mast amidships, stood looking abroad on the sea. Hardly anything of him was visible save his stiff fan-beard ; the rest was

16

wrapped away in oilskins. He looked like a big wine-butt covered with a tarpaulin—from which peers a head.

A knot behind came No. 2, and still a knot behind No. 1. All their for'ard hulls, except their stems, were invisible under foam. The water went clipping backward and upward from their rams with the brisk hiss of syringe-expulsion, while behind they left a region of spotless churned milk. Their crews for that day made up their minds for biscuits and cold things ; cooking was out of the question.

But by noon the *Huelva* had grown very small in the north distance. By one, when the coast of Grenada was made out by the big ship, the little ones had vanished, and the big was all but invisible to them.

It almost seemed to Dick P. Hocking that he was enduring this hardly tolerable life in mid-ocean on board that pulsing boat in vain. But he bated no jot of his speed. At two o'clock Grenada was well in sight. At three the little flotilla divided, one passing by the eastward coast and two along the westward, to meet at the north end.

But the eastward boat quickly spun round, and hurried back south and then west and north to rejoin the others. She had, to the surprise of her crew, sighted the *Huelva;* nor could the *Huelva* have been sufficiently near to make *her* out. This was the news with which she went straining back. It was boat No. 2, on board of which, at this time, was Petersen.

# CHAPTER XXII.

## THE BATTLE.

THE *Huelva* had passed to the eastward of the island, though St. George is on the west, for the reason that the east is never used on the northward route to Martinique, to which island she had the appearance of being bound. She thus hoped to elude the pursuing boats. At the moment when she was sighted she was all but stationary in the water; a ton or less of coal was all she carried.

The hours passed. Four o'clock, five, six. She waited for darkness. The sea, as generally round Grenada, was very unsettled. The *Huelva* rode the slow, big swells with a gallant nonchalance.

And now the sun dips, and, as his last segment disappears, it is night.

There is a sound on board the *Huelva*, the rattle of electric wires. She prepares to make for St. George. As her lights gleam abroad, already overhead is a black vault of stars.

But besides the stars there are other lights which claim attention this night—three more on the sea, yonder to northward, suddenly appearing, and they draw fearfully nigh.

Have ships life? So sailors tell. And, if life, then an instinct of death? So, too, runs the tale. The *Huelva*, as she is in the act of moving round to south, drives her head into a swell with such sudden and sullen fury, that the heavy rush of water breaks the arm of a man against the armour of the bow-gun, and souses all her forepart in a drenching baptism. A singular act for her.

There are certain conditions of the atmosphere and light in tropical countries in which things remote seem more remote than they are. When their nearness becomes evident, it does so with a certain effect of surprise.

And a feeling of surprise it was with which the captain of the *Huelva* all at once became aware that the three lights were within a knot of him. He made haste to communicate that fact to Appadacca, who, indeed, already knew that he was again being followed.

Appadacca replied :

'Husband your coal.   Make ready for a battle.   Rig torpedo-nets—now.   I will come on deck.'

He entered a species of boudoir, and in a moment came out masked and cloaked.   He rang the bell communicating with the priest's suite, and sat with knit brows till the priest appeared.

'Excuse me,' said Appadacca hurriedly.   'It is necessary for me to tell you that I am about to be attacked by some small American ships of war.   You will not be alarmed?   I hope not.   I am so sorry for the inconvenience, for your sake.   At least, you will not now be taken by surprise, if anything serious should happen.'

'Do you anticipate anything?' asked the priest, his face very white.

'It is within the possibilities, holy Father.'

'Then, my son, you shall have my prayers——'

'Thank you.   I cannot stay——'

'Do you, then, direct the battle in person?'

'Yes.   Farewell.'

He was gone.   Up he went, with steady, stately step, up to the hurricane-deck, into the conning-tower.

It was a good-sized room, cushioned and

velveted within—without, gleaming nickel-steel.
In the fore-surface, a circular glazed window,
giving view of a wide reach of sea ; around, a
multitude of knobs and telephone-mouths, communicating with engine-rooms, gun-casemates,
and every part of the ship.

Now there was no more flying. As he
entered the conning-tower, Appadacca ordered
his helm to port, and as the intense moonshine
of her two searchlights shot shimmering over
the water, the *Huelva* ran to meet her enemies.

They were not quite two minutes apart, and
at the end of the first, Appadacca tinkled the
bell connected with the fore-port casemate on
the main-deck. The light was shining full
upon a torpedo-boat not eight hundred yards
away, and, following instantly on the rattle ot
the knob, the *Huelva* sent out the sharply-
punctuated, jabbering row of a four-inch Hotch-
kiss over the water.

The sea, however, was so unstable, and the
target so small in size, that only one shell told,
carrying away a cowl. And herein was mani-
fested that shrewdness of Dick P. Hocking
which had given him riches, that when advised
to have torpedo-vessels built for him, he had
stuck manfully to his boats, pointing to an ac-

count which he had been studying of the
blowing-up of the ironclad *Blanco Encalada* on
the Chili coast by two small torpedo - craft.
' The smaller,' he had said, ' the better.   Small-
ness, strength, speed, and tubes—those are my
sentiments.'

And now he had all this, his tubes number-
ing twelve.

The three boats came on in a line abreast,
No. 2 in the middle, No. 3 to starboard, No. 1
to port, with an interval of half a mile.   The
*Huelva* almost immediately upon her first outbreak passed between No. 1 and No. 2.   And
as she did so, trailing her lights on her two
enemies, with a unanimous battery of both
broadsides she sent forth a red thunder that
shook her frame to its keel.

And at once mast and funnel disappeared
from No. 1, and, as the *Huelva* sped past, the
crews of the starboard guns sent up a cry of
pride, for the boat's bows were seen to be as
low as her stern had been.

But meantime two eighteen-inch Whiteheads,
with a speed of over thirty knots, are making
for the great ship.   On each side one is
marked, with outcry, with alarm ; and wide,
wild eyes follow the hurrying run of that
bruised water-weal, and catch glimpses of the

fatal, struggling, buffeted, yet headlong steel. Appadacca's eyes turn from one to the other with patient, eager scrutiny. It is an awful moment.

Suddenly he orders helm to port, for he has noticed that the port torpedo slackens, while the starboard races steadily through and over the impeding sea. So long is the agony of suspense that there is time to shoot from the military-tops, but no shot takes effect. The *Huelva* turns to port, and at once arises the outcry that she is making straight for the port torpedo, which has been deflected by a wave ; and as she returns to starboard through a frothing curve, the starboard torpedo is shooting close upon her ; and an instant afterwards it is observed, with heart-shrinking terror throughout the ship, that *both* torpedoes have been caught in the stern-wake of the vessel, and are converging, with absolute, inevitable certainty now, upon her. Then from every bosom bursts a sigh as the swift catastrophe comes ; the torpedoes, rushing in the ship's wake, both of them, close. They meet— they clash ; and four hundred pounds of gun-cotton rend the air with a bang of venom at which the heart faints and the whole sea-depth trembles.

But the *Huelva* is untouched, and torpedo-boat No. 1 has disappeared.

With that rude self-sureness which distinguishes Americans, the crews of the torpedo-boats had not been chosen, except in the case of their commanders, for their special knowledge of torpedoes, or special skill in handling them—only for their general skill and intelligence. Hence the torpedo of No. 1 had actually been fired from beyond range, which in no case exceeded 700 yards, and was about to cease its motion when taken into tow by the *Huelva's* wake.

And now it is only two to one; and Dick P. Hocking's brow wears a frown, as does the brow of Petersen. The result is not so sure as it seemed.

One torpedo beneath the keel of that ship will suffice; but to get it there?

The boats were fitted with a system of double lanterns, electrically worked by a key-board, for signalling; and, as the *Huelva* came raging back to the south, Hocking signalled:

'Give her all possible torpedoes this time.'

At that moment the *Huelva's* captain was speaking to Appadacca in the conning-tower. Coal at that pressure could not last two more minutes. He had told the engineers that if the ship could not keep speed she must be destroyed ; but——

And again came the boats to meet her, port and starboard ; but this time at such close quarters, that no sooner had the machine-guns in the tops commenced to crackle than every living thing on the decks of the boats was mangled, and their whole riddled surface presented an aspect of havoc. Still, as the *Huelva* was prone to pass between them, at a distance of less than 400 yards from No. 2, a navy of five ripping steel-needles set out to reach her, shot rather at random, but all in a fair way to intercept and end her. The first, by the merest agile seamanship, and a slight sheer to port, slipped astern ten yards from the screws ; a second was caught by a wave, and tossed aside in a whiff of spray ; a third was caught in a net. At that moment the speed of the ship was furious ; quite suddenly she seemed to hesitate, to give in, to lapse, to pause. The fourth touched her port beam, and there, for half a minute, hung swaying ; the fifth struck her after-armoured tube to starboard at the level of the belt.

At that supreme instant, while expectation stood in silent horror, there burst a hissing shriek from the boilers of No. 2, and men

were seen wildly leaping at random over the
side, through a wide seething of white steam ;
but instantly afterwards this explosion was lost
and a thousand times drowned in two monstrous, deep-throated shocks, swift-succeeding,
which were like the death-sobs of the fated
vessel. From both bow and stern, high and
wide over the sea, she cast her mighty fragments, while at once the speed of the wreck
stopped totally, and she was seen to have
settled evenly lower all round her hull.

She was still in brilliant light ; and as the
only boat of No. 3 capable of floating came
near from the rescue of the men of No. 2, only
four of whom were found, Dick P. Hocking,
sitting in her stern, saw, standing on the bridge,
a figure which he had twice in his life beheld
—a man in a mask and mantle, a man to whom
he owed a debt, whose name he did not know.

The next moment the man was hidden from
sight, the ship being now one heaven-high
cloud of angry steam, proceeding from her
quenched and screaming fires. In the sea
were hundreds of men, who had plunged into
the water to escape the unexpectedly swift
doom of the vessel.

She left them not much time. Her bow
lurched down to port, then, as if she were

MEN WERE SEEN WILDLY LEAPING.

[ *To face p.* 252.

being tugged opposite ways by spasmodic strings, she jerked herself sternwards to starboard, and in that position lay wobbling a little, as if to settle herself to comfort, the seas breaking all the time over her bulwarks; and so remained an incredibly long time— perhaps three minutes—till she suddenly skipped forward, dived, and disappeared.

And once more, at nearly the last moment, Dick P. Hocking saw that cloaked figure; and he leant forward, and he lifted his right arm, and he said:

'You see that man standing there high up on the bridge? Ten thousand dollars to every man in this boat if he is saved!'

But the offer was met by the men with a certain sulky dissentience.

'Saved, Mr. Hocking, sir?' said one. 'It wouldn't pay you or me to go an inch nearer that ship now. No salvation for him in this world.'

'Does every man in this boat refuse?' cried Hocking, in a voice that equalled the shrilling steam.

No answer.

'Come along, parson; *we'll* do it together!' roared Hocking. 'It's my own boat, any way, I guess.'

And he manœuvred himself ponderously forward, pushed away an oarsman, and in a trice was doing stroke to the bow of drenched and scalded Petersen.

And never in his life did Dick P. Hocking come so near so huge a danger. As the boat drew nearer the ship, she was suddenly dragged into the influence of a vast wheeling basin of sea. She twisted, shot, and in an instant went careering with intense speed round the area of the sunken vessel's suction. Happily, at a hopeless moment, there shot from No. 3 a light, illumining a whole section of the whirl-pool ; and, as the light glowed red on the water, Hocking, before he knew what he had seen, or realized what he did, so swift was his action, had put out his hand and grasped the collar of a man.

# CHAPTER XXIII.

## THE MARRIAGE.

TORPEDO-BOAT No. 3 entered St. George with a crowd of castaways, picked up beyond the region of the *Huelva's* suction. Among them were Father Pedro and Josef Campos.

Hocking, on removing the mask from the face rescued in the whirlpool, had seen with a profound shock—with a throe that was half wonderment and half gladness—the face of Appadacca. As for Appadacca, he remained in a faint.

Hocking found at St. George a steamer, which he chartered for New York, and with him took Petersen, Don Pedro, and Appadacca.

As for the war, his interest in it was over. He knew now how it would end ; if not this time, then the next time ; if not this century, then the next century, or the century after that.

It would end as the quarrel of Appadacca and himself had partly already ended, and partly was going to end, in victory for the Saxon, and in the Marriage, as Petersen had said, ' with all the fiddles of God a-playing,' between the Saxon and the Latin.

Even yet Hocking did not carry his idea of marriage in his own private case without difficulty ; there was the pride of Appadacca, the haughtiness of the priest.   But Appadacca was really conquered ; he and the priest between them could not muster ten cents in ready cash ; and Hocking left no humility untried, no intercession unmade, to bring about ' the marriage.'

One day Appadacca said :

' Mr. Hocking, you have carried your point. In your way you are stronger than I.   I admit myself conquered—with gladness.'

' Well, now you are talking, sonny,' said Dick P. Hocking.

And so it falls out that the house of Hocking has now changed its name to ' Hocking and Appadacca,' and that, whereas Hocking is the man for the big idea, the gross conception, Appadacca can plan the details of its execution with fine skill, proving himself in very truth a ' helpmeet.'

The execution itself is left in the hands of

Campos. Appadacca does not live at New York, nor anywhere in 'the States'—neither, for that matter, does Hocking, for where Appadacca is, lo, there is Hocking also ; and Appadacca is mostly in old seigneurial châteaux, breathing an air of ancient peace and culture and loveliness, where one, of one's self, gets to feel that a human creature, having the same external form as Plato and Shelley, and, in fact, made in the image of God, should never, never say, ' I reckon, guess, and calculate.'

A distinct improvement is perceptible in Hocking's whole manner of speech, of bowing, of carrying his neck, of bearing about his abdomen.

His body is getting narrower, because he eats less, and eats better ; his head broader, because he cannot be got away from the side of cultivated Immanuel Appadacca.

And Appadacca is getting in many ways wiser, stronger, truer to Nature and the facts of life, because he cannot be got away from the side of level-headed Dick P. Hocking.

Only, between Father Pedro and Petersen there is not quite the same harmonious reciprocity ; for these are theologians, seeking not so much to find truth, as each to prove that truth is on *his* side—neither suspecting the possibility that Truth probably inhabit quite other regions than the small elbow-room at *his* ridiculous side. However, even Petersen and the priest have derived mutual blessedness from the union ; they follow Appadacca and Hocking from château to château, and discuss ; but in their discussion is a note of greater suavity : the priest is less arrogant ; the parson less rawly obstinate and impossibly hideous. In time they will find out that both are eternally right, and both barbarously wrong ; and for each reason they will learn the secret of Love, which is the secret of Life.

THE END.

BILLING AND SONS, PRINTERS, GUILDFORD.

# Americans in Fiction

*A series of reprints of 19th century American novels important to the study of American folklore, culture and literary history*